"Am I doing it wrong?"

D0631052

Emma called over to him as he neared [illegible]
Mariana. Her lean body swayed in the saddle.
"You're scowling."

Of course he was. He wanted to drag her off her horse and see if those full lips were as soft as they looked when he kissed her. Instead, he was stuck teaching her how to stay on her horse before she risked her neck by performing unwise stunts on his property. Thinking about something happening to her only made him scowl more.

"Your hands are fine, but your seat is all wrong." Had it been a mistake to work with her?

"My seat." She forgot about her hand position and let the reins go slack as the horse halted beside him. "I didn't know I could mess that up."

He shouldn't touch her again. Not when the contact from the first time still supercharged the air between them. He hadn't gotten involved today because he wanted to hit on her, damn it. He was only trying to keep her from getting hurt.

* * *

Wild Wyoming Nights is part of
the McNeill Magnates series
from Joanne Rock!

Dear Reader,

I watched a TED Talk last year where the speaker shared that one-third of women are victims of domestic violence at some point in their lives. I began thinking of the bravery it takes to confront an abuser or find a way out of a toxic relationship, and that led me to the heroine of this story.

Emma Layton is three years removed from her troubled relationship when *Wild Wyoming Nights* begins, but the memories remain. Some women recover by burying the past deep and trying to forget. But Emma took a different path, finding healing in a career change that empowered her. Being a stuntwoman allows her to confront danger—and win. Sometimes we are surprised by our own strengths when life requires it of us.

I hope that romance novels help remind us all what good, healthy relationships look like. Love may not be full of hearts and flowers every day, but it should never hurt. Please reach out if you need to, and teach your daughters to seek out men who lift them up and applaud their strengths. True heroes are out there!

Happy reading,

Joanne

JOANNE ROCK

WILD WYOMING NIGHTS

If you purchased this book without a cover you should be aware that this book is stolen property. It was reported as "unsold and destroyed" to the publisher, and neither the author nor the publisher has received any payment for this "stripped book."

Recycling programs
for this product may
not exist in your area.

ISBN-13: 978-1-335-97168-5

Wild Wyoming Nights

Copyright © 2018 by Joanne Rock

All rights reserved. Except for use in any review, the reproduction or utilization of this work in whole or in part in any form by any electronic, mechanical or other means, now known or hereafter invented, including xerography, photocopying and recording, or in any information storage or retrieval system, is forbidden without the written permission of the publisher, Harlequin Enterprises Limited, 22 Adelaide St. West, 40th Floor, Toronto, ON M5H 4E3, Canada.

This is a work of fiction. Names, characters, places and incidents are either the product of the author's imagination or are used fictitiously, and any resemblance to actual persons, living or dead, business establishments, events or locales is entirely coincidental.

This edition published by arrangement with Harlequin Books S.A.

For questions and comments about the quality of this book, please contact us at CustomerService@Harlequin.com.

® and TM are trademarks of Harlequin Enterprises Limited or its corporate affiliates. Trademarks indicated with ® are registered in the United States Patent and Trademark Office, the Canadian Intellectual Property Office and in other countries.

Printed in U.S.A.

Four-time RITA® Award nominee **Joanne Rock** has penned over seventy stories for Harlequin. An optimist by nature and a perpetual seeker of silver linings, Joanne finds romance fits her life outlook perfectly—love is worth fighting for. A former Golden Heart® Award recipient, she has won numerous awards for her stories. Learn more about Joanne's imaginative muse by visiting her website, joannerock.com, or following @joannerock6 on Twitter.

Books by Joanne Rock

Harlequin Desire

The McNeill Magnates

The Magnate's Mail-Order Bride
The Magnate's Marriage Merger
His Accidental Heir
Little Secrets: His Pregnant Secretary
Claiming His Secret Heir
For the Sake of His Heir
The Forbidden Brother
Wild Wyoming Nights

Visit her Author Profile page at Harlequin.com, or joannerock.com, for more titles.

been so focused on nailing the job that she hadn't thought twice when asked about prior riding experience. While it was true she'd taken informal lessons as a teen on the property where her mother worked for the famous Ventura family, Emma knew she'd only been granted the job because of her connection to Antonio Ventura, the director. Not that she would see him any time soon. As a stunt performer for one of the more minor characters in the film, Emma served as part of the second unit on this location. That meant she answered to the stunt coordinator, while Antonio would direct the leads.

Both units were filming at the Creek Spill for the next two weeks, but Emma hoped and prayed the shoot would run over. She needed the work almost as much as she needed to be as far from Los Angeles as possible right now. Far, far away from her ex-boyfriend, due to be released from state prison tomorrow. This job had been a godsend, a boon that made her determined to exaggerate her limited horseback riding ability.

This morning, Emma and her assigned mare stood outside the pristine Creek Spill stables with five other body doubles and their mounts. All waited for instruction from Zoe Bettle, the stunt coordinator who also served as horse mistress for the film. Zoe, an accomplished horsewoman in her midforties with the body of an athlete, appeared to be in a standoff with a tall, impossibly handsome cowboy in a dark Stetson.

At least, he *looked* like a cowboy.

His broad shoulders filled out a fitted gray T-shirt tucked into faded jeans with creases bleached almost white where the fabric contoured to his movement and muscle. His boots had the distressed leather look that costume designers labored to replicate with sandpaper and acetone. But the weathered appearance didn't extend to the rancher's face. He had the square jaw, chiseled cheekbones and full lips a camera loved. Clearly, he was one of the lead actors—someone with enough clout to raise Zoe's hackles. Emma could tell by the set to her shoulders that she was not pleased with whatever the man had to say.

Already, Emma didn't like him. She needed her boss in a good mood today so Zoe would be forgiving of the mistakes Emma was sure to make. As it was, the woman appeared ready to fire the first stunt rider foolish enough to screw up. Emma tried to calm her nerves by stroking Mariana's soft gray muzzle.

"Fine." Zoe's last word had enough volume to reach Emma's ears. She turned toward the assembled stunt talent. "A change of plans today, ladies and gentlemen." She strode closer to them, her tall riding boots stirring up dust from the pasture. Although she was just barely five feet tall, she carried herself like an Olympic gymnast, her perfect posture and musculature outlined by tan jodhpurs and a bright red T-shirt. "Our host, Mr. McNeill, has expressed concerns about our *horsemanship*." She articulated the word with all the affront she must be feeling. "So

I have assured him we will slow down our training schedule to meet the ranch's safety standards."

Their host? Emma glanced back at the rancher she'd mistaken for an actor, seeing him in a new light. If he was responsible for this sprawling ranch with its well-kept fields and neatly maintained barns, he excelled at his job. The Creek Spill was like a minitown in the middle of nowhere, from its bunkhouse full of ranch hands to its on-site cooking facilities and dedicated water tower.

"Ms. Bettle, I think you misunderstood me," the cowboy called from where he stood near the freshly painted four-rail fence that separated the pasture from the paddock area.

The stunt coordinator ignored him. She folded her arms and glared at the talent.

"We will divide into two groups. Ms. Layton and anyone else involved in the race scene, please show Mr. McNeill how well prepared we are for the stunt." Zoe's eyes bored into Emma's, warning her not to mess up. "The rest of you, come with me. We will be working in the far pasture so as not to disturb the local horses while they 'adjust to our presence.'"

Emma's boss did not roll her eyes, but her tone suggested how much she wanted to. Two other stunt doubles—both men, both stronger riders than her—stepped forward with their mounts and headed toward the rancher. Emma started to follow them, keeping hold of the leather reins as she spoke soothingly to the mare at her side.

"Ms. Layton." Zoe stepped closer to her, voice lowered. Hints of an Eastern European accent came through. "Carson McNeill signed a unique agreement with the production company that gives him the last word on safety conditions here. Since the Creek Spill is a working ranch, we don't have the luxury of sending him on a two-week vacation while we shoot. We must make sure he's satisfied that we know what we are doing. Yes?"

Emma nodded. "I understand."

Impressing Carson McNeill was priority one if she wanted to keep this job. Her palms began sweating on the reins as she glanced at the cowboy who now controlled her fate. Why couldn't she be filming a fight scene? Or jumping off a building? Anything but horseback riding. No doubt Zoe recognized Emma was the weak link in the stunt crew.

She'd been warned.

While Zoe and the remaining cast members mounted for the ride to the far pasture, Emma urged her horse, Mariana, forward. Morning sunlight glinted off the creek in the distance behind the ranch owner. The whole property flanked the water on both sides for two miles. When she'd first arrived at the Creek Spill two days ago, Emma had been overwhelmed by the beauty of Wyoming with its endless blue sky, rugged cliffs and rolling hills dotted with wildflowers. Now the spectacular view narrowed to Carson McNeill, where he stood under the shade of a giant ash tree.

He appeared to give instructions to both men in her group, and the guys were mounted and riding away before she reached his side. Her pulse raced; she wished she didn't have to speak to him alone. She'd mostly conquered her demons where men were concerned. After the nightmare relationship with her former boyfriend ended three years ago, Emma had started training herself for this competitive profession to supplement her work as a personal trainer. Stunt work appealed to her need to be more sure of herself, and she'd fooled a lot of people into thinking she had already arrived at that goal.

Right now, she was more worried about Carson McNeill calling her out for a fraud where her riding skills were concerned. Without the men in her crew to hide behind, she would be making it easier for the rancher to see her weakness. But the idea of appearing weak steeled her spine as she walked over to him, giving her the shot of bravado she needed to pull this off.

"I'm in the race scene, Mr. McNeill." She tipped her chin up and braced her shoulders. It was her personal "ready" position. "What would you like to see from me?"

She had a degree in exercise science. She'd trained hard to be here. This man would not send her packing.

"Call me Carson." He just barely touched the brim of his Stetson, a cowboy tip of the hat.

"Emma Layton." She didn't offer her hand since she held Mariana's reins with her right one and it was slick with nervous sweat. In her left hand, she clutched the strap of her riding helmet.

Carson McNeill was even more compelling up close, where she could see past the shadows cast by his hat. His eyes were pale blue. A hint of dark hair escaped his hat, curling at the base of his neck. His gaze dipped over her briefly, inspiring a flare of unexpected heat along her skin even though she was thoroughly covered in a standard workout T-shirt with the jodhpurs and riding boots Zoe had provided.

"Nice to meet you, Emma. And I assure you, I didn't mean to start the day on the wrong side of your boss." There was a certain practiced charm about his smile. She bet he unleashed it on other women with great success.

Emma couldn't afford to be interested, despite that lick of warmth she felt along her skin. The sensation wasn't from the smile that was too automatic, but from the intelligence in those blue eyes. A shrewdness that told her there was more to the rich rancher than a handsome face and honed bod.

"Zoe knows stunts and horses as well as anyone." Emma had read everything she could find about the woman on her flight to Cheyenne, and she'd been impressed. "She's probably not used to having her judgment questioned."

"I don't question her horsemanship, only the skills of her crew members." His gaze moved from Emma to Mariana, and he reached to stroke the mare's nose. "In particular, I noticed yesterday during the workout that you appeared uneasy at times."

Her stomach dropped. She hadn't known she was being observed.

"Yesterday we were simply tasked with getting to know our mounts." Sweat broke out along the back of her shoulders, though it wasn't all that hot for August. A breeze stirred the mare's mane and made Emma's skin turn clammy. Her heart rate quickened. "I've never worked with a horse that uses so many specialty commands. She's highly trained."

"Unlike you." He reached for the bridle. "May I?"

His fingers brushed hers, the contact sparking unwanted heat despite how he'd just insulted her. Relinquishing the leather, Emma tamped down her anger, knowing she needed to smooth things over with him or Zoe would send her home.

"Mr. McNeill—"

"Carson," he reminded her, letting Mariana's lead dangle to the ground. "And you don't need to hold her so tightly. That's why she's rocking her head like that. She wants some breathing room."

"Carson." She took a deep breath and tried to calm herself. Seeing the way Mariana quieted, Emma could hardly argue with him. "Stunt work involves a wide variety of skills. While I may not be the expert horsewoman that Zoe is, I assure you, I am well qualified to scale heights, take a fall or drive a burning car into a building."

He folded his arms across his chest, seeming to take her measure. "But you're not working with a car or a building. You're working with a nine-hundred-pound animal with a will of its own, and that brings a whole new level of danger to the job."

"That's why the production company imports horses like Mariana. They're used to the rigors of filming and working with a variety of people."

"That doesn't mean you can waltz in here after a Saturday at the local dude ranch and expect to pull off a stunt on horseback."

Too bad she had to do just that.

"Then tell me, Carson." She looked him in the eye, unwilling to back down. "What do I have to do to prove to you I belong here? You name it, and I'll rise to the challenge."

Because whatever dangers Mariana and the Creek Spill Ranch held for Emma, they were nothing compared to the damage an angry ex could do if she went back home now.

Emma Layton was turning out to be an enticing distraction he hadn't anticipated.

Carson stared into her deep brown eyes, her gaze unwavering as she awaited instruction. She was scrubbed clean of makeup, her brown hair scraped back into a ponytail and wrapped into a haphazard knot. Everything about her said she was here to work, from the determined set of her full lips to the tense shoulders she's squared to him.

She was a half foot shorter than him, with the kind of lean muscles that dancers possessed. She was hardly what came to mind when he envisioned a stunt actor but based on her scowl, he guessed she might breathe fire if he spoke that thought aloud. With her long elegant neck and delicate features, she looked more suited for ballet than daredevil tricks, but to each his own.

Or her own.

The fact that he found her grit and determination incredibly appealing should not be on his mind right now given how much production the Creek Spill Ranch lost every day that shooting continued on his property. Carson had his overly cautious twin brother to thank for all the added clauses in the contract with the film company that said the McNeill family had the last word on safety for the duration of the shoot. Normally, Carson was the easygoing twin and Cody took care of being the hard-ass. But Carson had needed to step in and fill his brother's shoes. Cody had a lot on his plate with his girlfriend expecting a baby. And now they were dealing with a new crisis: Cody and Carson's stepmother was in a coma.

Paige had been in intensive care after a fall while

hiking in Yellowstone, putting the whole family on edge the same week the film company came to town. Making matters more complicated, just a day before the accident, Carson's youngest half sister, Scarlett, had received a blackmail note threatening to reveal some secret from Paige's past that would damage the family.

While hell broke loose all around them, Carson was left to oversee the Creek Spill, plus make sure Cody didn't overlook anything at the other major family holding, the Black Creek Ranch, while everyone took turns sitting with Paige at the ICU in Idaho. Thankfully, Paige was being transported to the Cheyenne hospital today, now that she'd shown signs of coming out of the coma.

Still, it definitely wasn't a good time to be noticing the sex appeal of Emma Layton, who stared him down as though she wished *he* was the one driving a car into a burning building. Preferably at full speed. More often than not, women found him charming. How damned ironic that the one woman to turn his head in recent memory looked like she wanted to take his head off.

"I want you to feel more at ease on horseback," he told Emma finally, reminding himself he was not the demanding, inflexible McNeill brother. "That will decrease your risk of injury considerably."

Once he felt assured of her competence, he would return to work. She was a professional, after all, and she had a stunt coordinator watching over her shoulder. The company was insured for this kind of thing and the ranch wasn't liable.

Except Carson had a conscience to answer to, and damned if it hadn't grown bigger with his ever-responsible twin out of the picture. Their own mother, an experienced rancher, had died from injuries sustained while trying to separate a bull from the cattle. Carson had been four years old at the time, and he'd been there, along with his older brother. Her death had haunted the family and changed their father forever. He knew all too well that animals could turn unpredictable.

Emma lifted her riding helmet and strapped it on her head. "I'm ready."

"I sent your two colleagues out to the arena to work on their leg positioning." He pointed out the track his younger brother, Brock, used to show and train quarter horses, a lucrative side business at the Creek Spill. "There's a training area beyond that, next to a tack shed. Let's take your horse out there and we'll start working on your hands."

"Her name is Mariana." She pointed toward the horse as he began leading the gray mare out to the training field. "And what do you mean about my hands?"

He took the quieter shady route behind the barn, his boots finding the worn grassy path that hadn't been trampled to dirt yet. He thought he'd been prepared for the added activity of a film production on his property, but he'd underestimated how much equipment and manpower it required.

"They're too stiff." He hadn't given riding lessons since Scarlett was a girl. "You need a more elastic hold that doesn't place extra pressure on the bit. As it is, Mariana will get confused about what you want from her if she feels like you're tugging."

"I'm a fast learner." Emma slanted a look his way, peering over the horse's nose. "Just tell me what you want to see from me, I'll do it. I can't afford to lose this job."

There was more to that story. He could hear it in her voice. See it in the hint of vulnerability in those dark brown eyes. And he regretted that he couldn't give her the reassurance she clearly sought.

Opening the gate to the training area, he waited until Mariana and Emma were through before he latched it behind them. "And I can't afford for anyone to get hurt on my property. I made it very clear to the production manager when I signed the contract that a ranch is a dangerous place. I won't allow you to continue if I think you're at risk."

She huffed out a breath, regarding him with frustration she didn't bother to hide. Hands on hips, she faced him.

"Every single thing we do in my business puts us at risk. In my last job, I once had to reenact a knife fight over twenty times before it was right. The take they liked best was the one where I took a slice to the right calf that sent me to the ER. That comes with the territory and I know that going in." Her cheeks flushed with color.

He'd hit a nerve. Or else just wounded her pride.

"I'm more concerned about head trauma. If your horse throws you—"

"I'm trained to fall the right way," she reminded him.

"For a woman who is concerned about keeping her job, perhaps you should listen more and interrupt less," he suggested mildly, even though she was beginning to get under his skin.

She pursed those full lips thoughtfully. Then her shoulders eased a bit. "You're right. I'm nervous and defensive, and that isn't going to help. What should I do first?"

He had to admire how fast she shifted gears.

"Hop on your mount and I'll show you." He watched as she placed a boot in the stirrup and swung her leg over. Smoothly. Easily.

He amended his earlier assessment of her skills. She had more in her background than a weekend at a dude ranch.

Quickly, he ran down what he wanted to see from her, starting with an explanation of what her hands were telling her horse. She practiced gripping the reins farther apart so she could feel the horse's natural movement, allowing her to stay in sync with the animal. While the horse trotted around the track, Carson stepped out of the practice yard to check in with the two male riders in the arena. They looked better, but Carson wasn't releasing them yet. He called over Nate—a ranch hand who'd been working closely with Brock and the quarter horses for more than a year—and tasked him with giving the riders a few more tips.

"Me? I'm no riding instructor." The younger man scratched his head under his hat as he stared out at the arena, planting a dusty boot on the lowest fence rail. "I train horses, not people."

"But if you had to give these guys a handful of tips to make sure they survive two weeks on horseback, what would you say?" Carson glanced back to check on Emma, who had slowed to a walk.

"I'd say I'd rather work the hot brunette." Carson followed Nate's gaze, and noted the appreciative grin pulling at his mouth as he watched Emma.

His protective instincts stirred, surprising him.

"Seniority has its privileges." Though Carson didn't plan on pursuing his attraction for the prickly stunt double, he needed to keep safe for two weeks, especially after seeing that vulnerable look in her eyes.

Then again, he wasn't ready to walk away yet, either.

"You're the boss," Nate told him agreeably, turning his attention back to the stunt actors riding circles around the dirt track. "But the dude on the left rides too high in the saddle. Guess I could pull off his stirrups. Get him to work on his seat."

Carson clapped Nate on the shoulders. "Good thinking. Whatever you can do. By the end of the week, they're going to be racing and fighting on horseback, so I'd like to do whatever we can to keep them in one piece."

Leaving Nate to take over with the men, Carson returned to the practice yard, his attention fully on Emma. The thought of her racing at breakneck speed in just a few days from now made him edgy. He didn't want to tick off the stunt coordinator any more than he already had, and he had to get back to overseeing ranch operations, so he didn't have time to interfere with the filming. But he wasn't impressed with the level of safety he'd seen on set so far.

"Am I doing it wrong?" Emma called over to him as he neared her and Mariana. Her lean body swayed in the saddle. "You're scowling."

Of course he was. He wanted to drag her off her horse and see if those full lips were as soft as they looked when he kissed her. Instead, he was stuck teaching her how to stay on her horse before she broke her neck performing unwise stunts on his property. The thought of something happening to her only made him scowl more.

"Your hands are fine, but your seat is all wrong."

Had it been a mistake to work with her? To get involved when he had a multimillion-dollar ranching operation to oversee?

Heat crept up his back as he stared at her, an amused smile playing around her kissable mouth.

"My seat." She forgot about her hand position and let the reins go slack as the horse halted beside him. "I didn't know I could mess that up."

He would have preferred crooning extravagant compliments in her ear about the tight curve of her ass, but that wasn't going to help her stay upright during a race scene. Tightening his hold on his control, he reached to touch her left hand, nudging it higher.

"You need to be aware of your body at all times. Right now your hands are sending a bad message."

Her eyes widened for a moment before she redirected her focus and moved her hands to the exact position he'd shown her ten minutes earlier. Away from his touch.

"Right. Like this." Her cheeks pink, she stared down at Mariana's head. "What else?"

He shouldn't touch her again. Not when the point of contact from the first time still supercharged the air between them. He hadn't gotten involved today because he wanted to hit on her, damn it. He was only trying to keep her from getting hurt.

"You're sitting too far back in the seat." His gaze veered to her hips as she edged forward. Saddle leather creaked. She used a hand on the pommel to inch along.

Killing him.

Making his throat dry as dust.

"Better?" she asked, her voice a quiet stroke to his ears.

He nodded. Then, forcing himself to finish the instruction since it was damned important, he touched the back of her thigh.

"Legs should be directly under you." He let go almost instantly, backing up a step.

Still, the feel of her—lean muscle under those body-skimming jodhpurs—imprinted itself on his brain. He would be tracing a lot more of her in his dreams later.

"Is this better?" Her voice took on a husky note that he told himself must be from the dust in the air and not because the touch affected her as much as it had him.

"Looks good," he managed. "Take a lap or two and see if you can maintain it."

She rode off in a hurry and it was all he could do not take off his hat and use it as a fan.

Damn.

He'd exchanged far more provocative talk—and touches—with willing strangers in bars that had left him cold. Why was this bristly, defensive stunt performer getting under his skin so fast?

The sooner he finished the riding lesson the better. He had a ranch to oversee, a family falling apart and a blackmailer to catch. Thoughts of Emma Layton would have to wait.

Two

Four miles into her evening run, Emma regretted the decision not to take the cast shuttle back to her lodgings at White Canyon Ranch.

She'd been in a hurry to burn off the keyed-up awareness she'd felt all day working with Carson McNeill and thought maybe she could jog away that hypersensitive energy. Now, her thighs burned with a soreness that no workout had ever given her before. As a personal trainer strictly for female clients, she had plenty of thigh workouts in her personal inventory. In the future, she'd have to start recommending a day in the saddle to women who complained about their inner thighs.

Slowing to a walk on the grassy path alongside

a fenced-in field between the Creek Spill lands and the guest ranch where second unit cast and crew members were staying, Emma checked her directions on the GPS. She'd asked one of the stable workers about the route she'd chosen, and he'd assured her the dirt road was good enough to drive on in a pickup truck. Running would be no problem. She'd thought she'd been well prepared, peeling off the jodhpurs and stuffing them in her nylon knapsack along with an extra bottle of water. She'd changed into a clean pair of cropped leggings along with the running shoes she'd packed for her evening workout. Her boots she'd left tucked in a corner of the tack room, at the suggestion of the ranch hand who'd told her about the path.

The sun was sinking low on the horizon, though, and it occurred to her that it was liable to be very dark at sunset. Not like her neighborhood in Studio City, where she could run at all hours of the night and still see because of the streetlamps. Taking a moment to stretch in the hope it would ease some of the stiffness in her muscles, Emma breathed in the scent of fresh air and wildflowers. The breeze stirred the tall grass inside the four-rail fence.

She was just about ready to start running again when the hum of an engine alerted her that a vehicle was heading her way. Her shoulders tensed. Yes, Emma had taken plenty of mixed martial arts classes, training that served her well in stunt work and helped to make her feel sure of herself in isolated places. Still, she couldn't shake some of the old fears. Her ex-boyfriend was a fellow fitness trainer who'd hit her in a public place, in front of a room full of witnesses after a kickboxing class he'd taught. He'd tried to play it off like he was giving her an extra lesson, but thankfully no one else in the class believed that. An off-duty cop had been among the attendees, leading to the battery charges that kept her ex locked up for almost three years.

She didn't want to ever need saving again, though. She tightened her ponytail and started a light jog that irritated her burning thighs.

As the sound of the engine drew closer, punching up her heartrate, she turned to see a two-seater utility vehicle with an open cargo bed in back. The compelling cowboy she'd been trying to excise from her thoughts sat behind the wheel.

Her fears dissipated fast.

Carson McNeill braked to a stop beside her. The tension inside her shifted from fright back to the attraction she'd been fighting all day. She told herself it shouldn't matter that she was red faced and sweating. But it was tough not to be aware that she looked like roadkill when he looked like he'd just had a shower, with his hair still damp and his face freshly shaved. He wore a white button-down with the sleeves rolled up and a clean pair of jeans.

She paused beside the vehicle, swiping the back

of her hand over her damp forehead. "You can't possibly be here to critique my form. On my own two feet, I absolutely know what I'm doing."

He didn't even crack a smile. "My foreman told me you decided to run back to the White Canyon."

"When running alone, it's a good safety practice to let someone know where you're going." She'd taken extra precautions. "I told Zoe, too."

His jaw flexed. She'd seen that look often enough today when she'd tried his patience. Now, the furrow in his brow said he was downright aggravated.

"Speaking of safety practices, how many times did I mention that a Wyoming ranch can be dangerous? That animals can be dangerous?"

"Several." Hot, tired and sore, she was beginning to feel her own patience fray. "But since I'm off the clock for the day, I'm no longer your concern."

"If you're on McNeill lands, you're my responsibility." He swiped his Stetson off the passenger seat and tossed it in the cargo bed behind him. "Get in. I'll drive you the rest of the way."

She didn't appreciate the command, but she also didn't want to antagonize a man who still had the power to send her packing. Besides, her legs hurt and twilight would turn to full dark soon.

The vehicle didn't have a door so she swung into the passenger seat while holding on to the roll bar. Carson revved the engine once she was seated with her safety belt buckled.

"Nice ride," she remarked lightly, hoping he wasn't going to hold this latest transgression against her during this extra stressful week.

She'd had multiple texts from her roommate and her mother reminding her not to answer any calls from unknown numbers this week. They were both worried about her, with her ex getting out of prison. As if Emma wasn't worried enough on her own. But she couldn't imagine how Austin would find her here. Hollywood made no secret of lead actors' whereabouts, but anyone looking for information about stunt roles, especially smaller roles like this one, would be hard-pressed to find it. Another bright spot was that Austin would have no idea she'd gone into stunt work, even if he wanted to find her.

Beside her, Carson remained silent while the stars popped out overhead. One. Two. And then a million. The sight was breathtaking. She craned her head back to stare straight up, but she didn't need to. Pinpoints of blue and white light blanketed the sky in every direction.

"Wow." She glanced over at her silent driver, wondering if he'd grown immune to the beauty. "I've never seen stars like this."

Maybe some of her wonder seeped through his frustration, because he slowed the vehicle, then stopped altogether, the engine rumbling at idle in the creeping night. They sat on a hilltop with meadows rolling out into the distance on one side, and a shadow of rocky cliffs and trees on the other. He snapped off the headlights to give them a better view and turned off the ignition. The engine ticked for a few moments and then went silent.

"It's amazing how much the lights of a city detract from the night sky." Carson tipped his head back, too, his hands resting on his sprawled denim-covered knees.

The right one hovered close to her leg, radiating a warmth she could feel. Or maybe it was the electric current of attraction that made her skin tingle that way beneath her leggings. She had been on a few dates since breaking things off with Austin but nothing serious. She definitely hadn't experienced the sizzling awareness she got from being around Carson. What a shame for her body to finally wake up again around a man she needed to impress with her professionalism.

"It's funny," she said, needing to break the intimate thread of silence between them, "because I always think I live in a quieter area of Los Angeles." She tried not to think about his knee next to hers. His hand close to her leg. But memories of the way he'd touched her earlier—shifting her thigh on the horse—sent a fresh surge of heat through her.

"Even in Cheyenne, you can't see the stars the way you can out here. There aren't many perks to ranching, but the night sky is definitely one of them."

Straightening in her seat, she peered over at him. The breeze turned cooler.

"You don't like your work?" She was curious about him, this man who allowed a film production company onto his property but couldn't really relinquish control. "After seeing you on horseback today, I guess I just assumed you were born in a saddle."

He'd ridden beside her briefly before setting her loose to try the track on her own.

"Almost." She thought she heard a hint of a smile in his voice. Or was that wishful thinking? "But I never imagined myself overseeing cattle at my age. Ranching is fine for my twin brother, but I thought I'd be riding rodeo into my thirties."

She hadn't known about the twin brother. Or the rodeo past. Still, she could relate to what he was saying. She felt him shift beside her, turning toward her. A gust of wind blew through her hair, flicking strands against her cheek.

"I never thought I'd be recreating sword fights or high-speed chases, either. But sometimes life takes surprising turns."

"I'll bet it's an interesting story how you got here, Emma Layton." Her name on his lips felt as intimate as a caress to a woman who hadn't been touched by a man in a long, long time.

The rush of heat through her veins shouldn't have caught her off guard—she'd been feeling it all day around him. She'd run four miles to try to escape it.

Even so, the magnetic force that seemed to pull her toward him was like nothing she'd ever experienced. Her shoulders shifted fractionally closer. Her knee brushed his.

She drew in a sharp breath at the contact, ripples of pleasure radiating out from the point where she touched him. She forgot what they were talking about. Couldn't think of words to say even if she remembered. There was only the moment and the man. The endless starry sky enveloping them like a dream.

Maybe that was why she found herself leaning even closer—it all felt surreal. Like a time-out from the worry and stress of her real life, where everything was suddenly simpler. Where kissing Carson McNeill seemed like the only thing that mattered.

Her hand landed on his chest. Warm. Strong. Inviting.

She splayed her fingers wider, wanting to feel more of him. Then she tipped her face up to his. She was close enough to see him well despite the darkness. His eyes locked on hers for an instant—like two stars close up.

And then his lips claimed hers.

Carson had been wrestling with the need to touch Emma all day. For hours, they'd been in close proximity, and the urge to kiss her had been there. Every. Single. Moment.

He'd resisted. Triumphed. Walked away from her

at the end of the work day, satisfied that he'd done the right thing.

But as soon as he'd spotted her treating his ranch like her personal gym out on the pasture road, her glossy brown ponytail swinging while she jogged, he knew his restraint was all out for the day. She'd worn right through it with her bullheaded determination to fake her way through a horseback stunt. Hell, she'd shredded it with her grit and bravado that rivaled any bull rider's.

So now when she tipped her mouth up to his, freely offering the taste he'd battled his conscience over all day, he didn't have a prayer of turning away. Petal-soft and strawberry-scented, her lips parted on a sigh, molding to his. Yielding sweetly. She skimmed her palm over his chest, sliding lower. He wrapped his arm around her, anchoring her against him, feeling the swell of her breasts as she eased nearer.

Wind whipped around them, stirring the scent of her fruity shampoo as tendrils escaped the ponytail and tickled his cheek. Hunger for more surged, hunger he couldn't possibly satisfy. He'd never had a woman affect him like this—so swiftly or so completely. Her fingers clenched around the hem of his T-shirt, her nails gently scraping his skin and arousing a whole other heat they couldn't possibly indulge…

"Emma." He blinked his way through the sensual fog, hoping he'd regain reason as he broke the kiss.

As it was, he simply tipped his forehead to hers, waiting to catch his breath. Her eyes stayed closed a long moment. When she opened them, she edged away even more.

"Sorry," she murmured.

His eyes were adjusted enough to the dark that he could see her run her fingers over her lips. The gesture made his insides twist with need.

"I wish you weren't. Sorry, that is. I'll be damned if I am."

He debated starting up the utility vehicle and flooring the gas until he got her back to her room for the night. Behind a locked door. But his stepmother was being transferred to the local hospital tonight, and he wanted to be there for his family when she arrived in Cheyenne.

"You wouldn't say that if you knew why I'm here." Emma tightened her ponytail in a gesture he'd seen her repeat often over the course of the day.

He'd be willing to bet she didn't let her hair down often. And yeah, maybe that made him want to crow with victory that she'd seemed to forget everything else with him just now.

"What do you mean?" He forced himself to focus on her words and not the leftover heat still sparking through him. Then he started the vehicle, knowing he needed to get on the road for the hospital soon.

"I mean, I'm not an up-and-coming starlet, in town because I'm so excited to further my career."

She hugged her arms around herself, sitting back farther in her seat.

"You're not trying to get ahead in your career?" He didn't follow what she was getting at. "Could have fooled me given how hard you worked today."

"Yes. Well, I want to keep my job. Desperately." She slanted a look his way as they skirted a patch of trees and neared the lights of the White Canyon Ranch. "But that's because I need to be anywhere but LA this week since my ex-boyfriend is getting out of prison tomorrow."

Carson tried to process that. He hoped like hell that the ex in question hadn't hurt her. But damn. Wouldn't that account for her level of determination not to be in California this week?

"I'm sorry to hear you were in a bad relationship," he said carefully. "And I'm glad to know why it means so much that you stay in Wyoming for the film. But that doesn't make me the least bit sorry I kissed you."

"There's relationship baggage, and then there's relationship kryptonite. I'm pretty sure a felon ex-boyfriend puts me in the latter category." She lifted her nylon knapsack off the floor and set it in her lap, as if she couldn't sprint out of the vehicle fast enough.

Carson slowed to a stop outside the deep porch of the huge log guest ranch, wanting to tread warily in this conversation, but also needing to reassure her that her past didn't change how he viewed her.

"Your ex being in jail doesn't reflect on you. Only on him."

She unfastened her seat belt with a jerky movement. She was upset and he regretted having any part in making her feel that way. He'd watched her overcome one challenge after another on her horse today, admiring her never-ending supply of resolve.

"He was in prison for hitting me." She looked at him, her gaze unwavering. "And once he's freed, he'll come looking for me. The last thing I want to do is drag an unsuspecting man into the drama."

She bolted from the car as if she hadn't just dropped a bombshell in his lap. By the time he shook off being stunned and set out to follow Emma, the screen door was already banging behind her.

Three

Emma realized she was being a coward the moment she got through the door of the White Canyon Ranch.

She'd kissed Carson and let that kiss carry her away. Then, when she acknowledged to herself how much she'd enjoyed it, she had panicked. She'd flung her past in the man's face and sprinted. If she ever wanted to move beyond the abuse, she needed to stop acting like this. Like she was ashamed and embarrassed about it.

More than that, if she was going to move forward with her life, she had to stop putting up smokescreens when a hot guy tempted her to take a chance on the opposite sex again. She had to take ownership of her feelings.

Forcing herself to stop, she pivoted on the toe of her running shoe before she hit the first step of the main staircase. She wasn't surprised to see Carson striding through the front door and into the huge foyer with cathedral ceilings.

Her pulse stuttered, then quickened. He'd been appealing, sitting next to her in the darkened vehicle under the stars. Here, in the light cast by the huge antler chandelier overhead, he stole her breath. His gaze locked on her as he closed the distance between them, and those blue eyes saw right inside her.

"Can we talk privately?" he asked, his expression concerned, his touch tender as he wrapped a hand lightly around her forearm.

"Sure." She nodded. "I was just thinking the same thing." Peering around the empty foyer, she set her knapsack in a window seat behind a floor-length curtain draped around a wooden pull back. Then she followed him back outside to the wide front porch that wrapped two sides of the building.

Although the guest ranch was full to capacity with cast and crew members this week, the property was relatively quiet now. Emma recalled seeing a bulletin on her phone that a charter bus had been scheduled to transport interested sightseers into downtown Cheyenne tonight for dinner and entertainment.

As Carson guided her toward the railing at the far end of the building, she decided to save him the trouble of asking her more about her past.

"That was wrong of me to spring on you," she said, leaning a hip into the railing while he turned to face her.

"On the contrary, I'm glad to know so I can make sure you're safe here." His jaw flexed as he stared down at her. "I'm just sorry you went through that."

"Thank you." She couldn't help but feel touched. His words sounded heartfelt. "It's not something I make a habit of sharing. But I guess I got rattled after the kiss, and felt like you should know."

"I'd like you to move to the Creek Spill, where I have top-notch security."

She noticed he didn't say anything about the kiss, which was probably just as well. Maybe he wanted to forget about that moment of heated craziness, too.

Her thoughts skipped ahead to her position in the cast and what he'd just said about her staying at the other ranch. "Do you mean I can keep this job? You don't plan on making Zoe send me back home?"

A hint of a smile pulled at one corner of his mouth. She remembered what it had felt like to kiss him and got a pleasant shiver just thinking about it. It wasn't going to be easy to forget what had happened between them.

"One thing at a time," he cautioned. Pulling his phone from his back pocket, he tapped in some commands. "I've got a family obligation tonight, but I can have someone help you pack your things and move you into a suite at the Creek Spill."

"That's so kind of you, but I don't need help—"

The warning look in his eyes stopped her protest. "Then consider it a favor for my peace of mind. From now on, you're my personal guest."

The seriousness in his voice made her wonder how personal a guest she was going to be. Plenty of the first unit cast members were staying on his property, so she assumed she would be housed with them. Still, it might make things a little awkward with Zoe and her second unit crew if she wasn't staying with them.

"I'm not sure if my director will think that's such a good idea."

Carson finished whatever he was doing on his phone and pocketed the device. Then he put both hands on her shoulders, causing a warm heat that made her insides flutter.

"Then you can tell her the rationale, or I will, but she's going to have to agree to the arrangement." His thumbs sketched a light touch along her collarbone, and her skin heated everywhere. "I just asked one of the White Canyon staffers to meet you at your room, and transportation is on the way. The attendant will help you with your bags and see you into the vehicle. You'll be met on the other end by my housekeeper, Mrs. Tillson. She'll show you the suite where you can put your things and will have dinner ready as soon as you arrive."

She tried not to notice the way she wanted to

sway toward him. No man had touched her this way in years. As for tending to her every need so thoroughly? No man had done that. Ever.

Emma reminded herself not to get used to it. As soon as filming was done, she would be back in LA, trying to carve out a life for herself while Carson McNeill would still be lord of all he surveyed in Cheyenne. She couldn't afford to get used to the sort of help he offered.

"That's more than generous." Blinking, she straightened away from his touch, needing to stand strong on her own feet. "Thank you."

He studied her for a moment longer before he gave a clipped nod. "I'd help you settle in myself but my stepmother has been in the hospital and my family is expecting me over there. I'll see you in the morning, though. Help yourself to anything you need while I'm away."

He moved toward the driveway where he'd parked his vehicle, but stopped when she didn't join him.

She was still stuck on what he'd said about helping herself. While he was away.

Did that imply he'd be...with her when he returned?

The breeze blowing off the hills made her wrap her arms around herself, as a chill set in from the sweat that had dried on her skin after her run. A chill...or a pleasurable shiver. She didn't know what she was feeling, but she knew she needed to get a handle on herself.

"What is it?" he asked, though he didn't move toward her.

"I. Um. Just wondering." Nerves skittered through her. "Where exactly will I be staying at the ranch?"

He frowned. "The bunkhouse and external buildings are filled to capacity with the ranch's employees and with the film's cast and crew. But there's plenty of room in the main house. You'll stay with me."

Carson couldn't stop thinking about Emma.

He sat beside his stepmother, who'd finally been transported to the Cheyenne hospital after a week in a medical facility nine hours away. She had been cleared for a flight on a fixed-wing medical plane at the family's expense so she could recover closer to home.

And she *was* recovering, according to her team of doctors, even if Carson couldn't see much improvement in her condition. At least she was off the ventilator now. And all three of his half sisters—Scarlett as well as Maisie and Madeline—had been in the room with her yesterday when she'd opened her eyes briefly, a sign Paige was pulling out of the coma.

That was why Carson didn't consider it disrespectful that his thoughts wandered to Emma so often in the hours that he'd been watching over his stepmother in her private room. The door was closed to shut out most of the sounds in the hallway. A nurse came in every half hour to check monitors and adjust IVs, but other than that, the room was quiet except for a gray clock ticking on the far wall. His half sisters had left to grab some dinner and change before Scarlett—the youngest of the daughters Paige had with Carson's father, Donovan—returned to relieve him.

Carson had plenty to worry about right now with overseeing the ranches, making sure the filming didn't interfere with day-to-day operations, and beginning a private investigation into his stepmother's past to see if there was any merit to the blackmailer's claim. Yet as he sat in the big gray lounger between the window and the hospital bed, what concerned him most was Emma.

He'd been floored by the idea of any man raising a hand to her. The thought still made him sick hours later. He wouldn't have been able to take his shift at the hospital tonight if she'd refused to settle into a suite at his house. Because at least now he had the satisfaction of knowing—thanks to a text from his housekeeper—that Emma was safely ensconced in his place, behind doors with a security code. She was surrounded by ranch hands who worked for him, plus a security guard he'd paid to ensure the equipment barns and horses under his care remained untouched for the duration of the filming.

Carson had already requested two more security

guards to start tomorrow. One to ensure Emma's safety. Another to patrol the grounds. They needed to keep a watch for Emma's ex, but it would also help the McNeill family to monitor for any new threats from their mystery blackmailer. Emma's past gave him a good justification for the additional security since his siblings had agreed not to tell their father about the blackmail note Scarlett had received during her visit to LA the day before Paige's accident.

As for Emma—no one was getting close to her on his watch.

Except for him.

The thought didn't just whisper across his consciousness. It roared and shouted. The kiss they'd shared had seared itself into his brain, making him realize that despite his good intentions where she was concerned, staying away from her for the next two weeks was going to be impossible. It would have been tough enough for him to keep his distance while they worked together on her riding. But now? All that combustible attraction was going to be front and center, 24/7.

But she had to stay with him.

He'd kissed her. Touched her. Shared her confidence. That made him want to protect her.

The wide door to Paige's room creaked open and Scarlett backed into the room, juggling a balloon bouquet, flowers and a brightly striped duffel bag.

Carson shot out of his seat to give her a hand, darting around the rolling table with a water pitcher.

"Thanks." Scarlett threw him a grateful smile, her long dark curls still damp from the shower. "I couldn't resist loading up on things at the gift shop since we couldn't bring the flowers from the other hospital with us."

Carson set the hot-pink roses on the bedside table before tying the balloons to a handrail against the far wall. "I'll make sure she gets more in the morning."

When he finished the task, he hugged his sister, hating to see her look so worn-out. Not that he'd tell her as much. She was a beautiful woman, but she'd always considered herself less attractive than her older sisters. It was something about looking more like her mother, whereas the rest of them took after their dad. Carson knew it was baseless nonsense. But Scarlett had once filled his favorite boots with rocks and flung them into an irrigation pond after he'd told her she looked like a cartoon giraffe. He'd been twelve.

And he'd learned not to tease her.

"How are you holding up?" he asked as he pulled away, taking an extra minute to look in her eyes.

As the recipient of the blackmail note, Scarlett had borne an extra burden before their mother's fall. She'd been given the message during a confrontation with one of the actors in *Winning the West* at a Hollywood nightclub. A guy she'd dated briefly. Scarlett had gone to LA, wanting to set the record straight with the dude before he showed up in Wyoming to do the film. During their argument, a man neither of them knew had slipped her the paper. The message implied that Paige had had a different identity prior to marrying Carson's father.

Scarlett had been caught flat-footed when Paige had the accident before she could share the information. She'd told her siblings in the hospital, but regretted not speaking up sooner, during the hours when Paige had gone missing the night before.

"I'm fine." She nodded, then went to work around Paige's bed, straightening the already straight blanket, fluffing the pillow behind her mom's head. "No news from the private investigator you hired to look into Mom's past?"

"No." Carson knew Scarlett hadn't been keen on the idea, but her older sisters had been worried about the danger a blackmailer presented. "But in all fairness, the guy has only just started making inquiries."

For the first few days after Paige's fall, her health had been the number one priority and the family's time had been consumed with that.

"Dad will be angry when he finds out." Scarlett paused in her busywork, turning worried blue eyes toward her brother.

In the quiet of the room, the balloons bumped one another as they swayed from the air-conditioning blowing through a nearby vent.

"No, he won't." Carson had watched his stern father crack under the fears for his wife after her disappearance and then her fall. And even before that, Donovan McNeill had been dealing with his own father's reemergence in their lives after a long period of estrangement. The stress of the last year had changed him. "He's got enough to bear right now just worrying about her. He texted me a little while ago to tell you he'll be in around midnight."

The fact that Donovan had texted him in itself told Carson a lot about how his father had changed. Carson had opened his home to his estranged grandfather, Manhattan-based resort mogul Malcolm McNeill, when the old guy showed up in Cheyenne. Donovan hadn't spoken to Carson for weeks afterward, refusing to acknowledge the billionaire father he'd bitterly cut out of his life decades ago. But now, Donovan seemed to have moved past that, too worried about his wife to care about the old grudge.

"Okay. Thanks." Scarlett dropped into the chair closest to the bed and held her mother's hand, careful not to bump the IV line. "How's the filming going at the Creek Spill?"

Thoughts of Emma filled his head. Her scent. Her touch.

The danger she was in.

"Everyone is still settling in." He wasn't ready to say anything about Emma when they'd only just met. No matter that he'd moved her into his house. "Shooting starts tomorrow, though."

Scarlett stared at him expectantly. Had his sister already heard rumors about him spending all day with a sexy stuntwoman?

"Damn it, Carson, don't make me ask. Have you seen Logan King or not?" She leaned closer, one of her dark curls falling onto her forearm.

"Sorry." He'd been so wrapped up in thoughts of Emma, he'd forgotten about her sister's tangled connection to one of the stars of the film. "I've been busy making room for the extra stunt animals they brought for this thing. When they wanted to house animals, I didn't realize they'd be high-strung Spanish dancing horses that needed a whole damn barn to themselves."

"Spanish dancing horses?" Scarlett grinned. "You mean like Andalusians?" At his nod, she continued excitedly. "They're some of the best-trained animals in the world. I doubt they're high-strung."

His thoughts strayed to Emma again, as he remembered her working on the complex commands with Mariana. The horses knew how to fall, roll and do a series of complicated jumps.

He'd started out the day worrying about how Emma would do with the animal. Now, he was far more concerned about how she'd fare with a bastard of an ex circulating among free men again.

Before he could respond to his sister, two nurses

entered the room, pushing a rolling cart between them. It amazed him how many different tests they needed to run on patients.

"I'm going to let you handle things," he murmured to his sister before kissing her on the cheek. "But I'll keep an eye out for Logan and let you know how the shooting is going tomorrow, okay?"

She nodded while the nurses moved the cart closer. "Sure thing, Carson. Thanks."

He didn't need to check his watch as he left the hospital room. He knew that Emma would be long asleep by now back at his ranch. But that didn't slow him down any.

He'd rest easier once he was at home, under the same roof with her, personally making sure she stayed safe. The fact that he would relive every second of that kiss in his dreams tonight was just an added bonus. And something he couldn't help.

Emma stood on the balcony of the suite Carson had given her long after dinnertime, staring out at the ranch under the rising moon. She knew the moon was the same size everywhere, but right here, where she could see it break over the horizon, it was a huge white spotlight turned on the Creek Spill. She wrapped her flannel shirt tighter around her to stay warm against the cool night breeze. She hadn't brought a bathrobe, so she'd put on the flannel over the pajama T-shirt she wore with an old pair of running shorts. Summer was warmer in southern California.

The balcony under her feet was made of smooth planks covered by a big woven rug in sunset colors. The wooden chairs were made of narrow logs, the knots still visible, the cushions as thick as her mattress back home. She'd switched off the lights in the room behind her so no one roaming around outdoors would see her up here.

Or at least they wouldn't see her well. She'd been drawn outdoors by that big glowing moon, but now that she was out here, she took a minute to orient herself. The main house overlooked stables and a lighted swimming pool, along with numerous barns and sheds, all landscaped and much of it fenced. The buildings she could see, however, were small compared to the stables and barns where the stunt horses were kept and where Zoe was staying with many of the other crew members. She'd read online that the Creek Spill and its neighboring ranch, the Black Creek, were a combined fifty thousand acres, an amount of land that had boggled her mind.

It made her wonder how the owner of all that property had time to watch her ride a horse today.

Carson had an army of people working for him. She understood that now after meeting his housekeeper, who had shown Emma her room. A maid had brought up her dinner, which had been prepared by a cook. Knowing there were so many people on staff in the house had helped her feel a little less awkward about sleeping in Carson's home. It wasn't as if she was alone in the house with him.

Deciding she needed to stop thinking and start sleeping, Emma was about to return to her suite when a shadow emerged near the illuminated swimming pool.

A very male shadow.

The heavy shoulders and narrow waist told her as much. But she'd spent enough time admiring that particular masculine physique today that she didn't have to guess who she was watching.

Carson McNeill had come home.

He stood at the deep end, facing the house. Facing her. She recognized his clothes from earlier; he must have just returned from his family obligation. She didn't move, not wanting him to see her.

Wanting to watch him a little longer.

But then he raised his hands and dragged his T-shirt over his head. The light from the pool glinted off the bare muscle of his arms. She couldn't see his abs in the shadows but her imagination supplied a picture of them just fine.

It was too late to shout down to him. Or at least, that was what she told herself. She seemed to have forgotten how to move, let alone speak.

His hand moved to his belt and he stepped out of his boots. Her mouth went dry when he reached for the button on his fly.

She gasped out loud when he stepped out of the denim.

That must have been what he heard. His head snapped up then, his gaze immediately finding her.

Her heart thudded so loud in her own ears she wondered if he heard that, too. Still, she couldn't seem to lift her eyes from the slim-fitting boxer shorts that hugged his hips.

"Emma?" His voice smoked through her, heating her skin from the inside. "Is that you?"

Four

There would be no slinking back to her room now.

Emma struggled to find her voice, flustered to her toes to be caught gawking.

"Carson?" She feigned surprise, as if she'd been standing at the railing staring at the moon and not the almost-naked gorgeous man in the courtyard. "I—er—didn't see you there." She cleared her throat to smooth over the cracks in her voice. "It's a little cool out for a swim, isn't it?"

She couldn't quite peel her eyes away from him. But it was dark enough he couldn't possibly tell exactly where she was looking. She hoped.

He grinned, his teeth a flash of white in the moonlight. "Spoken like a southern California girl. And no, it isn't too cold." He backed up a step, retrieving his jeans and shirt. "I thought you would have been asleep by now or I would have checked on you."

Moonlight played over his muscles as he slid the denim back up over his hips. The light in the pool cast a watery glimmer on his chest until he put his T-shirt on. Having him less naked helped her brain cells start functioning again, but she wasn't forgetting what she'd seen any time soon.

"I'm fine." She wondered what "checking on her" might have involved, though. "Mrs. Tillson made sure I had dinner and helped me get settled."

She noticed he left his boots by the pool as he jogged across the pavers to the wooden staircase at the far end of the upper deck. The deck that led to her.

Straightening, she remembered what she was wearing. A flannel shirt over an outfit she normally wore to bed. It was decidedly lacking in coverage. While Carson climbed the steps, she discreetly adjusted the waistband of the shorts, easing them a bit lower on her hips to cover the tops of her thighs before wrapping the flannel shirt around her again.

Her heart thudded hard against her chest as he strode closer, his steps light on the planked decking that lined the whole upstairs floor along the back of this section of the house.

"Are you sure there's nothing else you need?" he asked as he reached her, his gaze missing nothing.

For one heated moment, she allowed herself to consider the question. Then reason returned and she shook her head. "I'm all set. And I appreciate the hospitality. I certainly never would have expected you to—"

He waved off her thanks, leaning on the rail as he faced her. "Don't think twice about it. I will sleep better knowing you're as safe as we can make you here."

A different kind of warmth filled her at his kindness. "Thank you." She soaked in the comfort of his protection for just a moment. His caring. Then she remembered his quick exit earlier. "Is everything all right with your family? I'm sorry that your stepmother is in the hospital."

He looked out over the ranch for a moment, his jaw flexing. He nodded. "Things are better now. My stepmother has been in a coma since she fell in a hiking accident, but her doctors say she's coming out of it."

"I'm so sorry. That must have been frightening for your whole family." Her hand landed on his forearm. Squeezed. She had a tenuous relationship with her own mother, but she couldn't imagine life without her. Jane Layton was the only family Emma had since her father's suicide when she was three years old.

A cool breeze chilled her, sending a shiver up her spine.

"I just hope they'll let her come home soon. Worrying about her has really taken a toll on my father." Carson glanced over at her, frowning down at her bare legs. "You're cold. Let's find a spot to sit away from the wind for a minute and then I'll let you get to bed."

He palmed the space between her shoulder blades, steering her toward the seating area close to the French doors that led into her suite. As she dropped into one of the thick cushioned seats, he tugged a throw blanket off the love seat and laid it over her legs.

"It's okay. I'm too wound up to sleep anyway." She hadn't anticipated her ex's release from prison to churn up so many old insecurities, especially after the months she'd trained to feel strong and confident. She tucked the edges of the blanket—a soft wool blend—under her to keep the wind out.

"I ordered more private security starting tomorrow." He lowered himself into the love seat, putting him at a right angle to her chair.

His knee brushed hers through the blanket, and she remembered exactly what he'd looked like when he'd been moments from jumping in the pool earlier. Her gaze found his in the light filtering through the French doors, her skin humming with awareness beneath the layer of wool.

"Thank you. But you've already done more than enough. I feel safe here." She couldn't allow herself to live in hiding, continually running from old fears. She'd worked too hard to overcome them.

"Nevertheless, I don't want you to worry if you see a guard keeping tabs on you. I'll introduce you in the morning."

She hesitated, not sure how she felt about having someone watch over her all day. "I have an early call."

Carson grinned. "I'm a rancher. Early is all I know." His smile faded, his expression turning serious. "Besides, we're working together for some of the morning. A security detail can't keep you safe in a horseback stunt, but elevating your riding skills will go a long way toward that goal."

"I can be at the stables by ten." She wasn't ready to share the details of the rest of her day, which involved demonstrating a few moves for a knife fight assigned to two other members of the stunt cast.

Fighting, she was good at. No doubt because she'd spent an inordinate amount of her training time on mixed martial arts in the last few years.

He looked like he wanted to ask more. To insist she meet with his security guard first, but he simply nodded.

"I'll introduce you to Dax at ten, then we'll get to work." He shifted on the love seat, leaning forward as if he was ready to leave. "I'll let you get your rest then." His gaze held hers, making a spark leap inside her. "Unless you're game for a night swim?"

A shiver coursed through her that didn't have the slightest thing to do with the cold.

She shook her head, unwilling to get any more tangled up with Carson McNeill. "A good professional risk taker knows where to draw the line."

His blue eyes lingered on hers for a long moment. "Maybe that was my problem as a bull rider. I never could walk away from a challenge."

Her heart thudded faster. Harder. If he'd leaned any closer, she wouldn't have been able to resist kissing him. Tasting him again.

But he rose to his feet with a terse "Good night" and strode down the deck in the opposite direction from where he'd come. She watched him for a moment, long enough to see him open the next set of French doors beyond hers.

He would be sleeping close to her then. Which would give her plenty to think about while she lay in her bed. Alone.

Scarlett McNeill was not at her brother's ranch in the hope of sighting Hollywood's hottest up-and-coming young actor the next morning. Of course she wasn't.

She had permission from the film production company to take some footage behind the scenes for a promotional video the McNeills could use afterward to tout their properties. She had a legitimate reason to hover around the site of today's shoot. The fact that Logan King was going to be in the scene filmed on a high meadow north of the Creek Spill main house had nothing to do with it. She had recovered from her old crush on him.

Mostly.

Besides, she had already suffered the indignity of flirting with him, falling into bed with him and then having him ghost her. The last thing she needed was a reminder of how mortifying it had been to have her texts ignored for weeks. But her family came first, and this footage could help the White Canyon Ranch for years to come. The video would also give more visibility to her brother Brock's business of breeding and training quarter horses.

Still, as she checked the settings on her phone's camera app, it bugged her that she needed to be in close proximity with a man who'd treated her the way Logan had. She'd even traveled to Los Angeles a week ago to try putting the situation firmly in the past by telling Logan off in person. It should have been gratifying to give him hell on his home turf before he showed his face in Cheyenne. But he'd turned the tables on her by announcing he hadn't meant to ghost her. He'd just been on a difficult shoot in the Congo, at the mercy of the notoriously hard-nosed director Antonio Ventura, the same guy directing *Winning the West.* Ventura had demanded the young cast "bond" and taken away their cell phones for two weeks.

The excuse had sounded overly convenient at the time, but she had done an internet search when she got home and the stories she'd seen backed up what Logan said.

Then there was the mysterious message about her mother from that night.

"Scarlett." Startled out of her musings, she nearly dropped her phone in the meadow grass.

Logan King stood a few feet away in all his glory, with his chiseled jaw, dark brown hair and deep green eyes. He was dressed in period costume, like a cowpuncher from the Old West, with cotton trousers, worn leather chaps and tall boots. His white shirt was half-open and stained with dirt, his leather vest soft enough to mold to his chest.

How fitting that her gaze ended up there. Cursing herself, she shoved her phone in her back pocket and resolved to look him in the eye.

"Hello, Logan." She tipped her chin up, ignoring the urge to smooth her windblown hair from her face.

"I hope your presence here means you've decided to bury the hatchet?" He stepped closer and lowered his voice at the same time.

A conversation for her ears only.

She realized he probably knew the handful of others milling around the big camera set up on a wide rug nearby. There were two screens mounted inside a rolling cart full of electronic equipment, with a canopy over it to minimize the glare. She didn't recognize any other stars among the group, and guessed they were technical experts of some sort.

"I'm only here to film some video to promote the ranch." And possibly to mingle with the Hollywood crowd since she had every intention of leaving Cheyenne for good this fall to test out a career in acting for herself. It was a dream she'd deferred far too long to help out her family. "So no, I don't consider the hatchet buried."

"Even though I was hamstrung by a despotic director?" He glanced over one shoulder before continuing. "Wait until you meet this guy. He might have some critically acclaimed pictures to his name, but this is the last time I work with Antonio Ventura."

"He's that bad?" she asked, telling herself she was curious more for the sake of her future acting career than because she was tempted to give Logan a second chance.

But he smelled amazing as he stood beside her. Like soap and aftershave. A hint of leather. She breathed deeper, remembering how he'd dazzled her when they first met. They'd been in first class on a flight to the West Coast. She'd been taking a shopping trip for her mother's birthday. They'd flirted. Kissed. Had an incredible surprise night together. She had thought it was about more than lust, and grew certain the feeling was mutual when they messaged each other briefly afterward. Then he'd mysteriously stopped, the growing silence hurting her more each day.

What if his ghosting her had been out of his control?

“He’s arrogant, demanding and unreasonable,” Logan continued, bending down to snap a sprig of white yarrow from the stem. “If I hadn’t already signed on for this picture, I would have never worked with him a second time.”

His gaze traveled her face, lifted to her windblown curls. Then he slid the wildflowers into her barrette before tucking some of her hair behind her ear. She told herself to move away. But his touch still affected her. Made her long to bury that damn hatchet after all.

She might have done it, too, if she hadn’t remembered her sister Maisie’s suspicions about him. That Logan could have been involved with the mysterious third party handing her that blackmail note.

That Logan himself could be the one who knew something about her mother’s past and wasn’t afraid to use it for leverage against the McNeill family.

Do you know your mother’s true identity? You might be surprised to find out her real name. And to learn her marriage to your father was never legal. I will make trouble for your family if you continue your plan to let Winning the West *film on McNeill land.*

She’d memorized every word. And although she

could buy into the idea that Logan might want to stop the filming of *Winning the West*, she couldn't reconcile the man who'd just slid a flower into her hair with someone plotting to take down the McNeills. He was Hollywood's golden boy.

His past was the kind of story Hollywood loved. He'd traveled to LA from the Ozarks as a teen without a penny to his name, doing odd jobs until he turned eighteen. Then he'd gotten a GED and started working as an actor. Just two months ago, at age twenty-six, he'd catapulted from small-time fame to the A-list when his breakout blockbuster released, giving him enough wealth and fame that it simply made no sense to turn to blackmail.

"Seriously, Scarlett," he told her, tipping her chin up to look him in the eye when she didn't respond to him. "I know you're angry with me, and I don't blame you. But when you come to LA and start working, please don't take any jobs with Ventura. He's a tyrant."

The fact that Logan King—a celebrity on the cover of half the magazines at the grocery store checkout right now—was not only looking out for her, but that he remembered and actually believed she could be an actress one day, broke through the last of her defenses.

She didn't believe him capable of trying to blackmail her family.

"I won't," she promised, gathering up the hair still

blowing in her face and holding it in one fist. “And I would consider burying the hatchet with you if you help me with something.”

“Really?” The smile that teased his mouth made her want to kiss him. “Name your price, Scarlett McNeill. I’m so there.”

Her knees felt weak. Was it any wonder the man had won the hearts of every female demographic in the US? Maybe she was crazy for giving him another chance, but what if he could lead her to the blackmailer?

Two other actors arrived on the set, a makeup artist dressed in black trailing behind them, wearing a work apron full of cosmetic brushes. They must be getting ready to start the scene soon.

She kept her voice low. “I want you to help me find the man who passed me that note at the club in West Hollywood last week.”

His green eyes held hers. He frowned for a moment. “He was wearing the pin-striped jacket, right?”

“You remember him?” A tremor of excitement passed through her. Maybe she should have asked Logan outright about it sooner, but she’d been so fearful that he could have something to do with it. And, of course, then her mother had gone missing and had the accident in quick succession.

“I’ve seen him around before.” He nodded when one of the other actors called to him, acknowledging the guy by holding up a finger to indicate he needed a minute. "I can find out his name for you. But you have to do something for me in return."

"I'm already considering burying the hatchet," she protested. "I think that's plenty."

He shook his head, shifting closer to speak in her ear. "You have to let me take you out to dinner tonight."

The tickle of his breath on her ear made her skin tingle with awareness.

"I'm busy," she told him, so damn breathlessly he had to know how much he affected her. But her mother was still in the hospital, and family came first.

"Friday, then?" he persisted, wrapping one of her curls around his finger.

She had to lick her lips before she spoke, her throat dry as dust.

"Okay," she agreed, telling herself it was for the good of the family.

Knowing that was a big fat lie.

"I'll text you, but you have to unblock my number." He backed away as his cast mates called to him a second time.

She smiled to think he knew she'd blocked him. Maybe he really hadn't ghosted her on purpose.

"Deal." She got out her phone to take some footage behind the scenes for her video as Logan walked away.

Had she made a bargain with the devil? It wouldn't

be easy to ignore the heat simmering between them, but if Logan had any answers about who was threatening her family, she needed to find out everything he knew. She just hoped she didn't get burned in the process.

Five

Settling his hat on his head as he left the foreman's office the next morning, Carson went to the stables, dark mood lifting at the thought of seeing Emma. His meeting with the Creek Spill foreman had run long thanks to a dozen pieces of business that had cropped up because of the movie crew's presence. Deliveries needed to be delayed because of storage issues. Grazing field rotations had been interrupted in some places and field maintenance was on hold in others because the crew wanted to shoot in a meadow with tall grasses.

Carson had agreed to all of it ahead of time in an effort to placate Scarlett and Madeline, who'd made the best case for the promotional value of the film for the guest ranch. But Carson had also done it, in part, because his twin brother had been so stubbornly opposed to having anyone on his own property, the Black Creek Ranch. Carson had been happy to step in as the good guy and offer up the Creek Spill instead. Butting heads with his twin was second nature by now after a lifetime of not seeing eye-to-eye. Carson had to admit his brother may have had a point on this one.

Cody had been adamant about safety precautions on the ranch given the way their mother had died. Now that Carson had the safety of a movie crew and cast on his shoulders, he could see why. If he ever found time away from the Creek Spill again, he'd owe Cody the courtesy of telling him he'd been right all along.

Although, if Carson hadn't signed off on *Winning the West*, he wouldn't have Emma Layton sleeping in the bedroom next to his. He'd take that trade-off again, even knowing the headaches that would come with housing extra people, equipment and animals.

As he neared the stables on foot, his brother Brock pulled up in his 4x4 pickup with the horse trailer already hitched. He called to him through the rolled-down window.

"Carson. Do you have a minute?" Brock was dressed for a meeting, his black button-down paired with his good Stetson, as opposed to the battered hat and dusty T-shirt that he wore when he worked with the quarter horses.

Carson didn't see Emma near the stables, but the security guy, Dax, lifted a hand in greeting from where he stood near the arena railing.

"Sure thing. You have a delivery today?"

Brock nodded. Folding his arms across his chest, he stared out at the stable yard where the stunt coordinator was working on a jump with another rider.

"I asked a long-distance customer to take delivery early on a couple of horses so I could have a few days away from the movie madness." He gestured to the stable yard full of strangers, his elaborate forearm ink on display where his sleeves were rolled up. "I'll be the first to admit I wasn't expecting the carnival to come to town when we said yes to this."

"I was thinking the same thing this morning. It's just for two weeks, though." Something he needed to keep in mind where Emma was concerned. He wanted her, no question. And he couldn't afford to wait if she was heading back to LA that soon.

"I've read that movie productions are notorious for underestimating the timetable. Especially films this Ventura guy is associated with." Brock turned toward him and lowered his voice. "But more importantly, I wanted to ask if you've heard an update from the PI you hired to find the blackmailer."

"No." Carson had meant to check in with him today. "But it's been a week with no new demands.

Maybe the note Scarlett received was just a shot in the dark. A one-off from someone maneuvering to keep the production in LA."

Out in the practice arena, the horse and rider fell as one. Brock swore softly, his shoulders tensing until the horse and rider both popped back on their feet.

"That's damned impressive, even if it's hell on the nerves," Brock muttered before returning his attention to his brother. "And as for the blackmail note, it seems too specific about Paige to be a shot in the dark. Someone has dirt on her and thinks we'll pay to hide it."

Carson frowned. "And if she married Dad under a false identity, it means the marriage isn't legal. At first, I wasn't too concerned since Paige and Dad have been together for over twenty years. In most states, that would be more than enough to have their union legalized as a common-law marriage—no matter her name. But I looked it up. Wyoming doesn't recognize common-law marriages."

Brock's jaw flexed. He scrubbed a hand over his eyes. "I know. And that makes me wish we brought Dad in the loop so he could put a lawyer to work on that."

"I'll call the PI today," Carson assured his brother, clapping him on the shoulder. "And I'll tell Scarlett she's got to make it a priority to ask Paige about it the next time she wakes up. She's remaining alert for longer periods of time now."

"You realize there's a good chance the person who sent Scarlett that note in the first place is someone who is here now, actively involved with the film?" Brock's expression turned to a glower as his gaze swept the stable area.

"The thought has occurred to me." Carson didn't want to think about a traitor right under their noses. "But I hired more security." He pointed toward Dax. "In fact, I have a meeting with one of the new guys now."

"I'll let you get to it then." Brock backed toward his truck, the door newly painted with the ranch's logo. "I'm going to escape the mayhem and deliver one of my best two-year-olds to a ranch on the West Coast. Take my time. Maybe come home Sunday unless I'm needed back here?"

Brock looked so damned hopeful Carson had to laugh.

"We should be fine. I'll let you know how Paige is doing and if there are new developments."

He left Brock to find Emma, surprised he hadn't already seen her around the stables since it was after ten. He'd barely slept the night before, thinking of her in the next room over, dressed in her skimpy night shorts. Her bare legs had been all he could see until he'd covered her with the throw blanket, her toned muscle and creamy skin a feast for the eyes.

That visual, coupled with the memory of her kiss, had fueled enough fantasies to make him restless. Edgy. Ready to have her all to himself for a while. He wasn't going to bank on *Winning the West* staying in Cheyenne more than two weeks. He needed to make his intentions crystal clear where she was concerned.

But first, he needed to find her.

He approached the bodyguard still standing at the arena fence. "Dax, I had hoped to introduce you to the woman who will be your primary assignment, but I don't see her. Can you check with your colleague who worked last night and ask about Emma Layton? I told him to keep an eye on her."

Dax, whose scuffed boots suggested it wasn't his first time on a ranch, nodded as he withdrew his phone from his pocket. While he tapped out a text on the screen, Carson scanned the stable yard one more time.

What if he didn't see her because her ex-boyfriend had found her first? A sickening feeling chilled his gut. He knew he'd been low on security yesterday. But he'd hired more for today—

Relief hit him fast when he saw Emma rushing his way, her glossy ponytail bobbing as she double-timed her step. She was smiling, but something about her expression struck him as off. Nervous, maybe?

Or was that just his leftover worry about her?

"Carson." She darted around one of the film crew

pushing a big cart full of electronic equipment. "I'm so sorry I'm late."

"Is everything okay?" His gaze locked on her dark brown eyes. He reached for her, still sensing something wasn't quite right. She looked agitated, her attention jumping around the practice area.

"Everything is fine," she assured him, turning to extend her hand toward the bodyguard. "You must be Dax. I'm Emma, and I'm sorry I got held up."

Dax took an extra moment to finish reading something on his phone before he shook Emma's hand. "It's nice to meet you, Emma. My colleague just texted me that you were cut up pretty bad this morning. Are you sure you're all right?"

Carson's stomach dropped. Ice filled his veins.

"You're hurt?" A hundred ugly scenarios filled his brain. "Your ex—"

"No." She shook her head. "Nothing like that. I was just working on some fighting techniques—"

"You were fighting." Some of the iciness in his blood started to thaw. Her ex hadn't been involved. But if he had a megaphone at that moment, he would have shouted to everyone within listening distance that the film was canceled and they all had to go the hell home.

"It's just a scratch on my arm—" she began, pointing to the hint of a bandage peeking out from her long-sleeve T-shirt.

"Excuse us, Dax." Carson didn't take his eyes off Emma.

Now her expression—the agitation, the nervousness—made perfect sense. He tucked her under his arm and drew her away from everyone, toward where his own truck was parked.

"Carson, I'm fine." Emma laid a hand on his chest.

Was she honestly offering comfort to *him*? Damned ironic when he wanted to wrap her in cotton and take her far away from here. Reaching his pickup, he opened the passenger-side door for her.

"You'll be even better after you take care of yourself."

She didn't make a move to get in his truck. She folded her arms and glared at him. "I have to work on my riding today. You're supposed to be helping me get better for the race scene."

"We'll practice when I'm sure you're all right."

"My word isn't enough?" She looked ready to dig her heels in.

Clearly she didn't know how serious he was about this.

"Not when I've seen you throw yourself from one dangerous situation into another. No." He leaned closer when she still didn't move. Quietly, he spelled out her options. "The alternative is that I get Antonio Ventura on the phone right now, and tell him the deal is off because safety measures aren't being met."

Her eyes narrowed. Her lips pursed.

He guessed she was debating the merits of arguing further. But maybe she could see that he had no intention of backing down, because she huffed out a sigh and stepped up onto the running board of his truck instead.

"Where are we going?" Emma asked as Carson drove right past the main house.

She'd assumed that was where he was taking her. Enforcing a day off or something. But now, as the truck wound down the long access road leading to a county highway, she had to wonder what he had in mind. He drove underneath the wooden arch where a sign hung for the Creek Spill Ranch.

"Depends." He glanced over at her. "Do you need stitches?"

"Absolutely not." She debated showing him the cut on her right arm to convince him it wasn't a big deal. Instead, she laid it on the door's armrest. "I refuse to be stuck with needles just to humor you."

He nodded. "Then we're going somewhere quiet to have lunch. Food will help you recover."

Defensiveness prickled. "I'm a physical trainer, Carson. I'm very familiar with health, nutrition and recovery days—"

"Sorry." He reached across the truck and covered her hand with his. "I know you're well trained. It's just that I'm only now starting to recover myself from when Dax said you were cut up. The first thing I thought of was that your ex somehow found you."

The admission eased some of her defensiveness.

"I hadn't thought of that." She flipped her hand over and squeezed his, her skin tingling where they touched. "I'm not used to anyone worrying about me." She tipped her head back against the leather bucket seat.

Yesterday the connection she'd felt to him had been all sizzle and steam, hot attraction coming to life after her libido had been on a long vacation. Today, in light of his moving her into his house and worrying about her ex-boyfriend, she couldn't deny feeling protected. And yes, cared for.

"Worry isn't something I'm used to doing." He surprised her with a wry grin, and then let go of her hand to put both of his on the wheel. "Hell, ask anyone in my family and they'll tell you I've never wasted a minute thinking about tomorrow."

When they reached the main county road, he didn't turn toward Cheyenne, making her wonder what he had in mind. But she was more curious about what he'd said.

"That reminds me of something you said yesterday. I got the idea your twin brother is the born rancher, and you wanted a future in rodeo."

His grin faded. "I've been the reckless twin my whole life. Cody ran the ranch. I tempted fate on the back of a bull. It was a role I was comfortable with."

She straightened in her seat, not believing her ears. "You were a bull rider? And you give me a hard time about stunt work?"

The truck slowed down for a hay wagon spitting grassy bits at their windshield.

"I give you a hard time because I recognize how demanding your work must be. I know it takes guts and maybe—excuse me for saying so—a certain amount of crazy to risk your neck day in and day out." He cast a sidelong glance her way.

Emma mulled that over as he turned off the main road.

"I'm not sure if I'm more offended that you think I'm a reckless nutjob, or if I'm more surprised that you think you are." She tried to identify where they might be going, but the road held no clues. Tall grass grew on either side of the truck. Yarrow and hyssop flowers bent in the perpetual breeze.

The pungent scent of the yarrow filtered in through Carson's half-open window.

"I meant no offense." He sounded sincere as they drove under a sign for Black Creek Ranch. She recognized the name of the place. The film company had wanted to shoot here originally, but Carson's brother had denied the request. "But it takes a unique personality to put your neck on the line every day."

Unlike the Creek Spill, the Black Creek Ranch was quiet as they neared the main house. Three tractors worked in a distant field, and a couple of ranch hands whistled to three dogs that went chasing after them toward the stables. But there were no concession tents for roaming cast members. No camera crews setting up shots. No stunt riders working with horses.

"I don't consider stunt work risking my neck." She glanced over at him as he parked near a large pine gazebo with a handful of picnic tables underneath. "I think of it as a way to prove to myself, every day, that I'm tougher than what life doles out to me."

He switched off the engine and turned to face her. "I guess it shouldn't surprise me that your reasons for what you do are a whole lot better than why I kept bull riding."

She waited, the fresh air still blowing through the window, riffling Carson's dark hair. Seeing him in his gray T-shirt with the ranch logo, she couldn't help thinking about how he'd looked the night before, stripping off his clothes by the pool.

"Why did you?" she asked, wondering how she was going to stop herself from kissing him again.

She might have rebounded from the damage inflicted by her last relationship, but that didn't mean she was ready for a new one. Even though Carson couldn't be more different from her ex, she simply didn't have the emotional resources for…whatever it was Carson made her feel.

Still, her heart picked up speed as he turned his blue eyes on her. He didn't seem in any hurry to get out of the truck. Then again, it wasn't even noon yet, so she wasn't particularly hungry for lunch.

A different kind of hunger stirred, though, making her restless. Warning her that she played with fire by being alone with this man, who could make or break her fledgling stunt career.

"We all did it for a while. My brothers and me. We started the sport because our father told us it was a good way to learn respect for an animal." He dragged in a deep breath. "Looking back, I'm sure it was connected to our mother's death. She died trying to separate a bull from the cattle, and I think my dad wanted us to grow up aware of the dangers."

By throwing his boys on the back of a bucking bull? Emma's vision of his father shifted as she tried to envision the kind of man that would do that to his kids. "I'm so sorry you lost your mother."

She understood better than he knew, having lost her father at a young age. But she didn't want to lose the thread of what they were talking about. She touched his knee with the hand of her uninjured arm, the gesture of comfort bringing with it a heated awareness. Birds chirped outside the truck, the soft rustle of leaves blowing a testament to how quiet it was here.

"Thank you. We all dealt with it differently. Dad retreated into himself, not paying much attention to us for—a long time afterward." Carson's gaze dropped to where her hand still touched him. Then, gently, he picked up her palm and laid it between his. "I kept riding bulls for years after my brothers stopped because it felt like a way to even an unspoken score between my father and me. A way to prove I could take whatever he dished out."

She watched Carson lift her captive fingers to his lips. It was easier to let herself be distracted by the brush of his mouth along her knuckles than to feel the ache of empathy for a young man seeking a father's approval.

"What made you decide to stop?" she asked, breathless from the tender kiss.

Slowly, he lowered her hand to rest in his on the leather console between them.

"After one too many surgeries to repair fractures or torn muscles, my father showed up at the hospital with an ultimatum. Quit bull riding or quit the family." He shook his head, a wry expression twisting his lips. "Guess he'd been banking on all of his sons walking away long before then. And he made it clear I was being selfish to put rodeo before the ranch."

Emma wondered about the surgeries and repairs. How much pain had he endured to prove a point to a stubborn man? She gave his hand a squeeze. "Did you remind your father it was his idea in the first place?"

Carson laughed. "No, ma'am. One surgery a week was enough for me. Risking Dad's wrath didn't even cross my mind."

She knew he wasn't completely serious. But she suspected there was a grain of truth in what he said. His father cast a long shadow over his life.

"And now? Are you glad you walked away from it?" She wondered if he was happy.

A strange thing to wonder, perhaps, about a man who had so much wealth and power. But then her mother had worked in the home of the rich and famous Ventura family for many years, and she'd shared with Emma plenty of incidents that suggested power and privilege did not make them happy people.

Carson tipped his head to one side, studying her as he thought about the question. "I don't miss the thrills and the roar of a crowd nearly as much as I thought I would. Ranching may not be as exciting, but it's a whole lot more satisfying." He lifted a dark eyebrow, casting a sidelong look her way. "Although, this week has been plenty exciting, now that I think about it."

The heat in his gaze sent her pulse into overdrive, warning her she ought to open the passenger door and get some fresh air before the spark between them caught into full-fledged flame.

He still held her hand, though. Or maybe she was holding his. The touch seemed so mutual, so necessary, she couldn't be sure. Her whole body warmed just looking at him, the moment wrapping around her with sensual promise.

Words eluded her. Until a tiny, frightened piece of her psyche piped up.

"I don't think I can afford any more excitement in my life, Carson." The words felt disjointed, like a ventriloquist worked her mouth to make the statement happen. But they were wise. Smart. Even she could see that as her skin smoldered from wanting his touch. She forced herself to let go of him. To open the passenger-side door. "Not now. Maybe not ever."

Six

Carson understood that Emma needed time.

She'd made that clear two days ago, after she'd cut her arm practicing a stunt. He'd backed off then, recognizing that she was going through a lot between the stress of her ex being released from prison and her effort to improve her riding skills for the horseback scene.

Today, he stood well behind the film crew as Emma performed the race stunt flawlessly for a third time in a row. As she took direction from the stunt coordinator before running through the action for a fourth time, Carson saw a new confidence in her while she stood beside her horse. An ease that hadn't been there the first day they'd met, when she'd been scared of losing her stunt job.

He knew that the time was right to pursue her.

Emma wore period costume for the scene. She had on a long white skirt with a matching high-necked blouse, and a wig on to give her a dark braid that spilled halfway down her back. Leather boots and a leather vest with a gun belt completed her outfit. Apparently, her character was some kind of high-born frontier wife forced to fend for herself and her children after her husband's death. The guns weren't loaded in the scene—the only thing Carson had personally asked the crew about that day since he tried to stay out of the way for the most part.

But safety on the set was still his number one concern. And with Emma's most challenging scene over after today, he thought they'd both breathe easier. There would never be a better time to take her out. To convince her to spend the rest of her time in Cheyenne pursuing the heat that hit him like a flash fire when he was around her.

Ever since that day in his truck, he'd been avoiding her whenever they weren't working on her riding skills, trying his damnedest to respect her wishes. Now? He saw no more need to give her space.

She was safe. Well-rested. The cut on her arm was healing. Security kept watch for her ex, but so far there'd been no sign of unusual activity on the ranch. Tomorrow was her day off. So tonight, he planned to take her out to celebrate her successful completion of this challenge. He wanted to talk to her. Touch her. Know more about her.

The need for her ate away at him even when he wasn't around her, and he had to think she felt the same way based on how she shivered when he touched her in passing. How he caught her gaze following him when she thought he wasn't watching.

"Looks good, doesn't it?" The feminine voice at his elbow startled him, making him realize how all-consuming his thoughts of Emma had become.

He turned to see his sister Maisie wrestling her thick dark hair into a short ponytail. This past winter she'd had a razor-sharp bob, but it had grown out. Maisie never wore makeup unless she had a reason to dress up, and then it always surprised him how his toughest sister could turn into a bombshell. Today, though, she was dressed in her usual ripped jeans, worn boots and a T-shirt for a long-ago rodeo.

"What looks good?" he asked, rubbing a hand along the back of his neck where a tension with Emma's name on it had been riding him for days.

Maisie straightened. Rolled her eyes. "The scene. Isn't that what you're watching? Or is there some unsuspecting female out there about to come under the sway of the full-blown Carson McNeill charm?"

She turned her gaze out toward the fourth take of the race scene.

"I'm just making sure everyone stays safe." It was

true, damn it. “Dad and Cody will have my head if the ranch ends up in the news because someone got hurt out here.”

“Save the BS lines for someone who will buy them.” Maisie didn’t even bother looking his way, her attention trained on the horses. “Only women can distract my brothers to that degree. Although I will admit a stuntwoman isn’t exactly your regular type.”

The tension in his shoulders moved to his head. “I have no regular type.”

“That’s not true.” She turned toward him, a smug grin on her face. “Cody only dates women he wants to marry. You only date the kind you won’t.”

“Ludicrous theory.” He returned his focus to Emma, not wanting to miss her when she finished for the day.

“Except it’s true,” Maisie continued, managing to gloat in a matter-of-fact tone. “Which has given Cody the most boring dating career on record—going from one serious girlfriend to Jillian. Marriage is only a matter of time there.”

Carson said nothing, although he acknowledged the truth of Maisie’s words. Cody was seriously involved with Jillian Ross, the film scout who was now carrying his child.

“And you don’t pursue women, but they all flock to you just the same.” She folded her arms and glanced his way. “Which means, if you’re actively scoping out someone and getting all prickly about it, you're breaking your pattern. And it tells me this woman is different."

"You're fishing, and you're wrong," he told her flatly. Then, needing to change topics, he brought up a far more pressing issue. "Any word on your mom? Has Scarlett asked Paige about the note yet?"

Over by the camera crew, he heard the stunt coordinator call for the cast members to run the race scene one more time.

Beside him, Maisie nodded, letting herself be distracted by the new question. "Mom's doctors might let her come home tomorrow if she continues to do well. Knowing we need to tell Dad soon about the letter, Scarlett and I sat down with her yesterday to show her the note and see what she knows about it."

"And?" He tensed, wondering why no one had phoned him. As the point person for the family's contact with the investigator, he expected to be kept in the loop. "The PI needs to know what she said if we want him to find out the truth."

"We learned nothing concrete," Maisie assured him. "Mom turned ten shades of white and called for a nurse."

Carson swore softly.

"I know. We felt terrible for pushing her, but between you and me, I'd guess there was some truth to the accusation in the note, or it wouldn't have upset her so much."

"If you bring it up again, make sure you stress to

her that we love her and don't care about her past. We just need to know who might want to use the information to hurt the family." Carson might have issues with his father, and some with his twin, but he would do anything to protect his family. "I have the feeling we'll hear more from the blackmailer soon enough."

"I hate the idea that it could be someone we're hosting." Maisie hugged her arms around herself. "You remember whoever wrote that note didn't want the filming to happen here in the first place, so they must have something to do with *Winning the West*."

"Did you warn Scarlett to be careful around that actor?" Carson had put Logan King at the top of the list of people to investigate since his youngest sibling had a history with the guy.

"I did, but I don't think she listened. I saw them together yesterday."

"His past is shady." Carson knew that much from the PI. "Except for a younger sister who went into the foster system and got adopted, his family members are all in jail or dead."

He couldn't let Scarlett get hurt. He had enough reasons to regret letting the movie crew onto his property. The safety risks. The slowdown in ranch production. Ticking off Cody and his father, which—despite what they might think—hadn't been his primary objective in offering use of the ranch.

But as Carson peered back out over the meadow where Emma was riding hell-for-leather on the back of her gray mare, he acknowledged there was still one reason the he wouldn't trade the decision for anything.

When Emma finally finished the last take on her horseback riding scene, she was ready to run a victory lap.

She'd stayed on Mariana's back successfully despite the speed of the gallop and the other horses crowding her. She hadn't flipped over the mare's head any of the times the horse had to make a quick stop and turn, which was the other tricky part of the stunt.

With the thrill of triumph still in her veins, Emma slid to the ground and patted Mariana's neck as she looked over to the place where Carson had stood watching her for most of the filming.

Disappointment stung when she didn't spot him. It surprised her how much she was looking forward to sharing this moment with him. It was his success as much as hers, considering how hard he'd trained with her these last few days to keep her safe.

She told herself it didn't matter. She'd asked him for more space after that day in the truck when she'd been ready to come out of her skin from wanting him. So she could hardly hold it against him now that he'd done as she'd asked.

Handing off Mariana's reins to one of the handlers, Emma went to the wardrobe tent, where she changed out of her period garb, retrieved her phone and purse, and turned in her skirt and blouse to the costume mistress. She'd worn simple khaki shorts and a white tank underneath, so changing was fast. Before she went back outside, she decided to check her messages. There were a couple of other cast members running in and out, but Emma had a quiet corner behind a rolling rack to herself.

There were a handful of texts from her mom that she'd look over in a minute. But the one that caught her eye first was from Carson just a few minutes ago.

You rode like a pro! Celebration dinner under the stars at 7:00? I want to show you a new view.

The thrill of anticipation that shot through her was like nothing she'd ever felt for another man. The promise of passion was a lure she couldn't resist. Not with Carson. Besides, she was free from her past—she deserved to seize the moment with a man who treated her well. He applauded her strengths even as he tried to protect her. He gave her the space she asked for, even when he could have used the simmering heat between them to overrule her common sense.

Continuing to deny the attraction hadn't made her feel stronger. If anything, it made her worry she hadn't fully recovered from her past so that she could take this kind of risk. Still, her fingers trembled just a little as she typed out a response.

Yes.

She hit Send and barely had time to exhale before his response made her phone chime.

I'll meet you in the courtyard of the main house at seven.

She would be alone with him tonight. Desire smoked through her at the possibilities, yes. But she couldn't deny that the emotional risk scared her. Giving herself a minute to slow her racing heart, she tried to read her mother's long, rambly texts.

Tucking one foot under her, she scrolled through the messages, skipping past some of the drawn-out worries about Austin finding Emma again. Emma had spent enough of her own energy fearing that without allowing her mother to wind her up again.

Jane Layton had been diagnosed with bipolar disorder after Emma's father committed suicide, and her mom had been on medications ever since. She'd been in a long depression for much of Emma's childhood, but the last five years had been full of mood swings, manic episodes followed by prolonged crashes. Emma tried not to add to her mother's stress, so she needed boundaries for how much she shared about her own life.

However, she couldn't remain quiet for too long, or she'd add to her mother's anxiety. It was a constant tightrope walk to help her mother stay level.

From what Emma could glean from the long texts, her mom's latest fear was that the McNeill family was going to take advantage of Emma. Mom had read about the family online and was worried they were entitled and privileged. There was a long rant about how money did not equate with honor. Another text compared the Venturas—the family who'd employed her mother for decades—to the McNeills, with some discussion of how rich people used others for their own ends.

Emma finally switched off the screen in the middle of reading a text, unwilling to get sucked into baseless fears. She'd been in family counseling more than once, with her mom and by herself, to learn strategies for coping with this kind of thing. And right now, when Emma had just enjoyed a professionally rewarding day, she reminded herself that it was okay if she didn't respond yet. She would enjoy tonight with Carson, savor the triumph of the race scene and then reply tomorrow. In the morning, she would craft a calming, neutral answer.

Still, as she walked back to the main house to get ready for her night out, she couldn't help feeling a sense of foreboding. Because sometimes, at the heart of her mother's outsize fears, there was something legitimate, which always made it difficult to discount them completely.

What had her so upset about the McNeills?

From what Emma had seen, they were generous

to allow a film crew so much access to one of their working ranches. She hadn't met Carson's brothers or half siblings, but she'd gathered they were a tight-knit group who operated connected businesses. And as for Carson…

Her heart galloped faster at the thought of their upcoming date. Slipping into a back door of the Creek Spill's main house, Emma hurried to the stairs to reach her room. Tonight clearly wasn't about working together to keep her safe on the back of a horse. Carson's celebration seemed entirely personal.

And no matter what her mother might think of the McNeill family, Emma trusted Carson enough to be alone with him. That was more than she could say for any man she'd met in the last three years. Was it so wrong to want to enjoy this moment of feeling like she'd made progress in her journey toward healing?

The door to her suite was open, the way she'd left it this morning. But it was clear someone had been inside. A stack of crisp white boxes rested on the brown leather sofa in the sitting area, the name of an upscale women's boutique written in block lettering on each one. The smallest of the pile was a thin, flat package, crisscrossed with bright blue ribbon.

Sticking out from the ribbon at an angle was a card with her name scrawled in bold penmanship. When she flipped it over, there was a message:

Pulling out all the stops to celebrate. If you want

to set aside your boots for a few hours, I picked out some things I thought you might like.

Intrigued, Emma slid a finger under the ribbons and pulled them off. She opened the box to find a delicate platinum chain, the loops so fine they looked like lace. At the center was a pendant of diamonds in the shape of a horseshoe, the polished stones cut to refract light in every direction. Her finger trailed over the jewelry, hardly daring to believe he would give her such a gift.

She couldn't keep it, of course. But she also couldn't ignore that kind of thoughtfulness. She would wear it to dinner and enjoy the feel of it on her neck. For this brief window of time, she would celebrate the way the McNeills did—with extravagance.

A thrill shot through as she turned to see all the other gifts stacked up and waiting. Excited to see what each one held, she pulled out one beautiful thing after another. A white crepe top that looked like it would bare her midriff. A full-length black silk skirt with a daring slit up one leg. Tiny diamond hoops for her ears. Bright teal-colored high heels with straps that went around her ankles. A tiny satin drawstring bag to carry her things—black on one side and teal on the other so she could choose which to use.

There were silver combs for her hair. A designer makeup kit in a travel size.

Everything she could possibly need to feel glamorous.

It was perfect. Exciting. And the only cloud hovering over her evening was the knowledge that her mother sat alone somewhere, worried that Emma was going to be taken advantage of by the rich and powerful McNeills. What would Jane Layton say if she saw the way her daughter took her time showering and applying her makeup for a date with her host tonight? The way Emma slid into that black silk skirt and felt like the most sensual creature on earth?

No doubt, her mother would tell her to run.

But Emma had been doing that for three years straight. Tonight, she was done hiding. With the thrill of a successful stunt behind her, she hoped she had the courage to take the one risk she hadn't dared in all that time.

Carson's breath stuck in his chest when Emma stepped out of the house dressed for the evening. He'd been sitting by the pool while he waited for her, messaging the private investigator and checking in with his sister Madeline about Paige's condition.

But one look at Emma's thigh through the high slit in the black skirt she wore had his brain scrambling like he'd just been bucked off a two-thousand-pound bull.

He gave an admiring whistle and shoved his phone in the pocket of his tux jacket.

"Well, thank you." She tucked a flyaway hair behind her ear, the diamond hoops glinting in the sinking sunlight. "You've got some good taste, Carson McNeill."

"I only chose the date and the horseshoe necklace." He edged past a lounger to meet her at the end of the pool deck. "But I agree, my taste in those things is outstanding."

Seeing her now, with strawberry-colored gloss slicked over her lips and something shimmery on her eyelids, made him realize she hadn't worn makeup any of the times they'd been together before. She didn't need it any more than she needed silk clothes and diamonds, but she carried herself differently tonight. And he liked that a whole lot.

Offering her his arm, Carson led her down the wide stone path toward the car he'd rented.

"Then who chose all these beautiful things for me?" She kicked out a foot to show off her bright blue shoe. Pink toenails peeped through the straps. "And it all fits."

"My half sister Madeline runs the guest ranch where you were staying before you moved over here. When I asked her about her favorite boutique, she quizzed me until I told her your name. She remembered you from check-in."

"I remember her, too." Emma paused in front of the limo. "What's this?"

"Our ride to the airfield." He stood back to let

the driver open the door for her. "I didn't think the pickup would cut it."

"Airfield?" She bit her lip.

His gaze tracked the movement, and the desire to taste her became a tangible need.

"There aren't many options for fine dining nearby. I thought a night in Jackson Hole would be nice."

Plus, taking her away from the ranch and Cheyenne meant a night off from worrying about her ex finding her.

"A benefit of being a McNeill." Squaring her shoulders, she stepped into the limousine and slid into the plush leather seat that wrapped around the back corner of the vehicle.

Carson settled into the seat beside her while the driver shut the door and put the car in motion. He reached for the champagne in the ice bucket.

"Ready to toast your success?" He spun the bottle so she could see the label to make her decision.

"Actually, as a personal trainer, I try to walk the walk with what I tell my clients and really limit alcohol intake."

"I respect that." He tucked the champagne back into the ice. "But I can't let it stop me from making a toast." Reaching past the silver bucket to the mini fridge, he found a bottle of sparkling water and cracked it open. "It's important to celebrate milestones."

The limo pulled out onto the main road. Carson

noticed that traffic was heavier than usual in the other direction. But then, it was Friday night, and there were more visitors in town than normal with the film shooting here. Everyone else was headed downtown for an evening out, making him glad they were driving toward the private airstrip instead.

"Here." Emma leaned forward to retrieve the crystal champagne flutes. She held one out for him to fill, then the other.

Her bare knee grazed his as she shifted on the seat. Her light lemongrass scent drifted toward him, making him want to get closer and find the places on her skin where the fragrance hid. When she leaned back into her seat again, he realized he'd been holding his breath.

Damn. What a powerful effect she had on him.

He clutched the base of his champagne glass, the chill of the water reaching the stem as he lifted it. He told himself to keep the focus on a friendly celebration. To give her time to enjoy herself. She deserved that.

"To you, Emma. To your grit, your daring and your skill. You impressed me all week with your commitment to improving, but I admired you most today, when I saw you ride the stunt over and over again like you'd done it a hundred times."

She laughed, shaking her head like she could wave off the praise. "You don't know how scared I was."

"I do." He'd seen how hard she worked to get better. And he thought he understood the nuances of what drove her to keep this job. It wasn't just about avoiding her ex, but triumphing over that chapter of her past. "That's what made it so special. Cheers to conquering the challenge."

Her gaze turned serious. "Cheers."

They drank at the same moment, gazes locked until Emma glanced away. She set aside her champagne flute as the vehicle turned. Through the tinted windows, he saw a handful of private planes. Two of them were on the tarmac, ready for departure.

His plane—his grandfather's Learjet that he'd welcomed the family to use while he stayed in Wyoming—and another that Carson didn't recognize.

He did recognize the woman standing near the jetway, however.

"Isn't that one of your sisters?" Emma asked, sitting forward while the limo rolled to a stop, kicking up a small cloud of dust on the gravel parking area. "And she's with Logan King." Emma's hand squeezed Carson's arm lightly. "One of the lead actors."

Carson knew damn well who Logan King was.

And even though his date was the most compelling woman he'd ever been with, it still took superhuman willpower for him not to sprint out of the limo ahead of her to ask the guy just what the hell he thought he was doing.

Seven

Of all the luck.

Scarlett had to resist the urge to chew on her freshly painted fingernail as her brother Carson stepped out of his limousine at the private airfield. Her brothers never went anywhere. What were the odds one of them would suddenly decide to take a Friday night flight at the same time Logan had invited her to Los Angeles for the dinner date she'd promised him?

Carson charged toward them now, his lovely date having to double-time her steps to keep up. The woman clutched the side slit of a stunning silk skirt with one hand while Carson bore down on them.

"Do you know that guy?" Logan asked, his arm sliding protectively around Scarlett's waist.

His touch—instinctual, automatic—was a pleasant counterpoint to a situation that was going downhill fast.

"It's my brother." She glanced up at Logan while their driver stowed their overnight bags on board the aircraft.

"Scarlett." Carson sounded just like their father when he broke out his stern voice. "Going somewhere?"

"Hello to you, too." She turned her attention to the tall, beautiful creature by his side, who must have been involved with the movie. The woman had amazing legs and the bearing of someone used to being in front of the camera. "Excuse my brother's manners. I'm Scarlett, the youngest sister, who will forever be stuck at thirteen years old in his eyes."

"Emma Layton." The woman had a strong, friendly handshake. Warm but no-nonsense at the same time. "Nice to meet you. That's a great dress."

Scarlett would have returned the compliment and gladly swapped fashion notes if her brother didn't take a menacing step forward, his gaze locked on Logan.

"Carson McNeill." He thrust his hand toward Scarlett's date.

But Logan appeared prepared. He released his hold on Scarlett to shake her brother's hand.

"Logan King." He sounded relaxed, but Scarlett could see the tension in his shoulders as the two men shook. "I invited Scarlett to dinner in LA tonight."

The muscle in Carson's jaw worked, and Scarlett guessed that she had Emma's presence to thank for his restraint as he appeared to weigh his words.

"When will you be home?" he asked, a warning note in his voice.

Scarlett drew a breath to defend herself and her life choices, but Logan answered smoothly.

"Scarlett hasn't decided when she wants to return, but I'm hoping to talk her into staying through Sunday, so she can meet my sister." Logan turned to Emma. "I saw some footage of the race scene stunt on one of the actor's phones. Great job."

Scarlett laid a hand on Logan's chest. "Logan, would you and Emma excuse my brother and me for just a second? I know we're scheduled to take off soon and I just want to give him an update on Mom."

"Of course." Logan squeezed her hip just slightly as he said it. A touch of reassurance. But oh, did it make her remember their night together—and so much more. "I can ask Ms. Layton how she managed to stay upright on that horse."

Scarlett smiled gratefully at both of them before she clamped a hand on her brother's thick wrist and drew him to one side.

He followed her, his thunderous scowl like a raincloud ready to burst. He held his peace as she stalked away from the metal steps leading to the jet door. When they got closer to the nose of the plane, the engine rumbling loud enough to mask their conversation, he stopped and leaned toward her.

"Are you out of your mind?" he asked, his expression shifting from pure Neanderthal to brotherly concern.

Her heart softened. "I know you're worried about me, but you don't need to be. I don't buy the theory that he's the blackmailer, okay? And furthermore—" she put a hand over Carson's lips to forestall the argument he had ready to roll "—Logan remembers the guy who passed me the note in the first place, and he's going to help me find him this weekend."

When she lowered her hand, Carson retorted, "So he says."

"And *I* believe him. So you're going to have to go out on a limb and trust my judgment because I'm getting on this plane with him, not that it's any of your business."

Her brother rocked back on his heels a bit. She didn't think for a moment it meant she'd won her case. Only that he needed to regroup. In that moment, she saw beyond the argument, to the man beneath. She reached up to smooth a wrinkle on his lapel.

"You look handsome, by the way," she admitted, adjusting his bow tie even though it was already straight. Her brothers were hard men, but she knew they'd been raised by a demanding father. Her mother had been good to them, but Paige had never been able to shield them from their father the way their birth mother might have been able to. Paige had deferred to her husband on everything where Carson, Cody and Brock were concerned.

"Thanks." Carson kissed the top of her head absently. "And blackmail aside, sweetheart, I just can't help but think this guy hurt you before."

She tipped her head against her brother's chest. "There's a good chance I misread what happened." Levering away from him, she looked up into his eyes, which were reflecting the bright lights of the airstrip. "And I like him enough that trying again is a gamble I'm willing to take."

"I just wish you were having dinner here. Close to home."

Stubborn, stubborn man. She peered past him to see Logan showing Emma something on his phone. Still, she couldn't leave him to make small talk all evening. She looked her brother in the eye.

"I need this break, the distraction. Do you know the kind of pressure I've been under at home lately, Carson? My mother's been in a coma and I've barely left her bedside. She's weak and confused, freaking out when I try to ask her about her past. Plus the stress of not telling Dad about that note is tearing me up inside." She clenched her hands in frustration. "I feel like it's all my fault he wasn't told to start with, and every day we keep it from him—"

"Hey." Carson took her hands in both of his. Held them. "It's not your fault. We decided as a family that's what was best. For now. I will be the one to tell him when I get back tomorrow."

"You would do that?" Scarlett hadn't realized until just now how much that task weighed on her. But having Carson lift it away made her feel lighter. Relief rushed through her.

"Of course. This is on me." He hugged her shoulders and turned her around, back toward the metal steps leading up to the jet. "Take the weekend to recharge, but I want to hear from you if you learn anything from this guy who passed you the note about Mom, okay?"

"I will," she promised, keeping pace with him as they headed back toward their companions. "And I hope you're extra nice to Emma tonight now that she's seen your overprotective side."

"Was I that bad?" he asked, his eyes glued to the tall brunette.

Interesting. Women always noticed Carson, but he'd never given his heart to anyone as far as she could tell. Dates came and went for her brother, whose attitude toward women had always been easy come, easy go, and Scarlett had comforted more than one of his disappointed ex-girlfriends who'd thought there was a chance with him.

That he was concerned what Emma Layton thought of him—heck, that he was taking her somewhere on a *plane*, for that matter—meant she was special.

"She had to sprint like an Olympic runner to keep up with you when you were storming over to me," Scarlett observed lightly, taking just a little sisterly pleasure in his obvious worry. "But I'm sure you'll woo her well."

He grumbled something about Emma not being "like that," but by then, Scarlett had reached Logan's side.

She was more than ready to think about the night ahead as her absurdly handsome date turned his green gaze her way. Her heartbeat stuttered, her breath catching in her lungs. She knew she needed to be very careful around him if she didn't want to get burned a second time.

Still, as he reeled her closer, sliding an arm around her waist and dropping a kiss on her temple, she knew it wasn't going to be easy to stay strong.

"I missed you," Logan whispered into her ear while Carson led Emma toward the McNeill family jet parked nearby.

Tamping down the desire to lean more fully into him, Scarlett straightened and met Logan's gaze, determined to hold him to their bargain. He'd find the man who passed her a blackmail note if she shared a meal with him.

"I believe you promised dinner?"

* * *

Midway through an exquisite meal served by the private wait staff on the deck of Carson's mountainside home just outside Jackson Hole, Emma was still trying to shake off a sense of foreboding.

The evening had been picture-perfect, starting with their timely touchdown in Jackson Hole after the short flight from Cheyenne. A driver had greeted them at the airfield, and delivered them straight to the chalet Carson kept for weekend getaways, a beautiful property with breathtaking views of the Teton Mountains. Even by moonlight, the vista from the back deck was impressive.

The huge patio had been stocked with extra outdoor heaters in deference to the dip in evening temperatures here. But Emma wasn't the least bit cold, between the warmth from the heaters and the fire burning in the outdoor fireplace. And, of course, the ever-present burn of awareness for the man seated beside her. Carson had appealed to her in denim and boots when they had worked side by side at the Creek Spill. Tonight, she saw another side of him: the worldly business mogul whose holdings stretched far beyond Wyoming. From the tuxedo he wore with casual ease, to the multiple homes and staffers, Carson McNeill was an influential man who could order the world to suit him.

He had the meal catered by the local Four Seasons, and Emma had her choice of entrees prepared in the kitchen on-site. The wait staff had greeted them formally, ushering them to the outdoor table laden with candelabra and hors d'oeuvres.

Emma's salmon had been delectable, then their waiter had recommended the pistachio mille-feuille and lavender ice cream for dessert. Emma had no clue what a mille-feuille might be, but she was game to try it, especially if it helped take away the sense of unease brewing inside her ever since they'd run into Carson's sister Scarlett and the actor Logan King.

"Are you enjoying everything, Emma?" Carson asked, leaning forward in his chair. "You seem quiet."

They sat next to each other at the round patio table draped in white linen. They'd moved aside the candelabra—each flame housed in a tiny hurricane lampshade—to clear their view of the shadowed mountains and the dark hiking paths that Carson said would be ski trails once the weather turned.

"The meal is wonderful." She appreciated the effort he'd gone to for her. "I can't imagine a more extravagant celebration for today, and I am truly grateful to you for helping me keep my job."

A breeze off the mountain threaded around her legs, tickling the silk of her skirt against her calf.

"And yet, you've been lost in thought." He seemed to have heard the unspoken reservation in her voice. He reached across the table to claim her hand, threading his fingers through hers. "Are you worried about anything?"

Her mother's texts. A niggling fear that the McNeill family might have more in common with the domineering Venturas than she'd first thought. But she knew that wasn't fair to Carson, who had been kind and thoughtful, extending his home and protection to her during a stressful time in her life.

"I've been thinking about your sister, actually," she hedged. It was partly true, at least. "Scarlett."

He shook his head. "She told me I needed to make it up to you for coming across like a Neanderthal tonight."

"She said that?" Emma couldn't help laughing.

"Not in those exact words, but close enough," he admitted. "In my defense, I've been worried about her. She had a relationship with that actor before and the guy—" Carson huffed out a breath between his teeth. "I don't know what happened, but I know she was hurt."

"So you had reservations about her taking off with him for the weekend. I can see why." Emma thought back to her conversation with Logan. "Although if I had to guess, based on the way he kept glancing over at her, I would say he genuinely likes Scarlett."

Carson didn't appear reassured. He leaned back in his chair as the waiter returned with their desserts. Hers was a culinary work of art, the pastry layers delicate and flaky looking, with whipped mascarpone and pistachio between the layers. Carson had a pavlova—a meringue cake with Chantilly cream and berries. As the waiter left them to enjoy the treats, Emma picked up her fork to try the pistachio filling.

Carson watched her, his blue eyes following the movement of the silver tines as she swirled them through an airy layer of her dessert. "May I ask what made you think of my sister?"

"Oddly enough, a text message from my mother." She put her fork back down, unsure how to convey her concerns. "My mother is a perpetual worrier, and she's been messaging me often this week—as you can imagine—wanting to be sure I'm all right."

Carson gave a half nod. "I can see why she'd be concerned for your safety. But what does that have to do with Scarlett?"

Absently, Emma adjusted the diamond horseshoe pendant where it fell on her neck, a reminder of Carson's thoughtfulness, which gave her courage to share some of her mother's personal battles.

"My mother suffers from a combination of bipolar disorder and anxiety, so her fears can be excessive. But she's scared I'll get sucked in by the McNeill world once I have a taste of the finer things." The note from her mother did seem prescient, given the over-the-top private celebration Carson was treating Emma to tonight. "I know it's because she had an affair with her wealthy employer long ago, and there was a time when she thought it meant something to him." As a young child, Emma had seen her mother fall into a deep depression and it had been terrifying.

Carson listened patiently, even though she hadn't yet made the connection to his sister that he'd asked about. Drawing a deep breath of the clear mountain air, she leaned forward in her seat.

"I guess she thinks that power and influence can seduce people who've never had either." *Like me.* "And maybe she has a point. But I keep thinking your sister Scarlett grew up in that world of wealth and privilege. Yet she's been drawn in by someone like Logan King." It was true enough, Emma thought. And now that she was knee-deep into the conversation, she had to acknowledge she'd waded in with the hope of voicing her worries for herself, too.

Was she in over her head with Carson?

He studied her for a moment before he swiveled on the seat of his chair, turning fully toward her. Covering her hand with his, he squeezed her fingers gently.

"Scarlett has always wanted to be an actress. I think that's some of the reason Logan's world fascinates her. But Emma, if I've made you uncomfortable tonight, or if you feel like I've made any kind of assumptions about where this is headed, I apologize." His gaze was steady. And, if she had to guess, sincere. "We can get back on that plane anytime and return to Cheyenne. No harm, no foul."

"No." It surprised her how much she didn't want

"FAST FIVE" READER SURVEY

Your participation entitles you to:
✶ 4 Thank-You Gifts Worth Over $20!

Complete the survey in minutes.

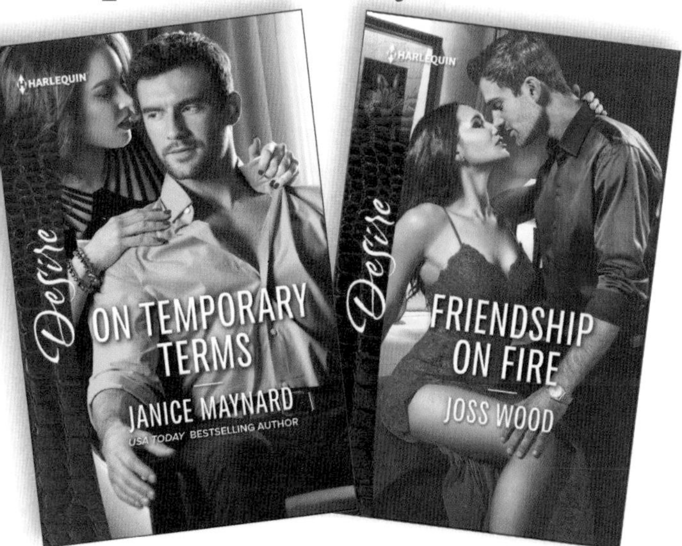

Get 2 FREE Books

ɔur Thank-You Gifts include **2 FREE** **'OOKS** and **2 MYSTERY GIFTS**. There's ɔ obligation to purchase anything!

See inside for details.

Please help make our
"Fast Five" Reader Survey
a success!

Dear Reader,

Since you are a lover of our books, your opinions are important to us... and so is your time.

That's why we made sure your **"FAST FIVE" READER SURVEY** can be completed in just a few minutes. Your answers to the five questions will help us remain at the forefront of women's fiction.

And, as a thank-you for participating, we'd like to send you **4 FREE THANK-YOU GIFTS!**

Enjoy your gifts with our appreciation,

Pam Powers

www.ReaderService.com

To get your 4 FREE THANK-YOU GIFTS:

* Quickly complete the “Fast Five” Reader Survey and return the insert.

▼ DETACH AND MAIL CARD TODAY! ▼

“FAST FIVE” READER SURVEY

1. Do you sometimes read a book a second or third time? ❍ Yes ❍ No
2. Do you often choose reading over other forms of entertainment such as television? ❍ Yes ❍ No
3. When you were a child, did someone regularly read aloud to you? ❍ Yes ❍ No
4. Do you sometimes take a book with you when you travel outside the home? ❍ Yes ❍ No
5. In addition to books, do you regularly read newspapers and magazines? ❍ Yes ❍ No

YES! I have completed the above Reader Survey. Please send me my 4 FREE GIFTS (gifts worth over $20 retail). I understand that I am under no obligation to buy anything, as explained on the back of this card.

225/326 HDL GM3T

FIRST NAME | LAST NAME

ADDRESS

APT.# | CITY

STATE/PROV. | ZIP/POSTAL CODE

Offer limited to one per household and not applicable to series that subscriber is currently receiving. **Your Privacy**—The Reader Service is committed to protecting your privacy. Our Privacy Policy is available online at www.ReaderService.com or upon request from the Reader Service. We make a portion of our mailing list available to reputable third parties that offer products we believe may interest you. If you prefer that we not exchange your name with third parties, or if you wish to clarify or modify your communication preferences, please visit us at www.ReaderService.com/consumerschoice or write to us at Reader Service Preference Service, P.O. Box 9062, Buffalo, NY 14240-9062. Include your complete name and address.

HD-817-FF18

® and ™ are trademarks owned and used by the trademark owner and/or its licensee. Printed in the U.S.A.

READER SERVICE—**Here's how it works:**

Accepting your 2 free Harlequin Desire® books and 2 free gifts (gifts valued at approximately $10.00 retail) places you under no obligation to buy anything. You may keep the books and gifts and return the shipping statement marked "cancel." If you do not cancel, about a month later we'll send you 6 additional books and bill you just $4.55 each in the U.S. or $5.24 each in Canada. That is a savings of at least 13% off the cover price. It's quite a bargain! Shipping and handling is just 50¢ per book in the U.S. and 75¢ per book in Canada*. You may cancel at any time, but if you choose to continue, every month we'll send you 6 more books, which you may either purchase at the discount price plus shipping and handling or return to us and cancel your subscription. *Terms and prices subject to change without notice. Prices do not include applicable taxes. Sales tax applicable in N.Y. Canadian residents will be charged applicable taxes. Offer not valid in Quebec. Books received may not be as shown. All orders subject to approval. Credit or debit balances in a customer's account(s) may be offset by any other outstanding balance owed by or to the customer. Please allow 4 to 6 weeks for delivery. Offer available while quantities last.

If offer card is missing write to: Reader Service, P.O. Box 1341, Buffalo, NY 14240-8531 or visit www.ReaderService.com

BUSINESS REPLY MAIL
FIRST-CLASS MAIL PERMIT NO. 717 BUFFALO, NY
POSTAGE WILL BE PAID BY ADDRESSEE

READER SERVICE
PO BOX 1341
BUFFALO NY 14240-8571

to go home tonight. Now that she'd allowed herself to think about going through with this—being with Carson—she didn't want to back out of it. "I mean, I may be having a few jitters about tonight, but I definitely want to be here."

He lifted her hand to his lips and brushed a kiss along the knuckles. She would have never thought of knuckles as an erogenous zone, but...wow. The sizzle of awareness hit her bloodstream like a whiskey shot.

"I'm glad to hear it. And I'm sure Scarlett can take care of herself."

Emma wanted to believe him. But something Logan had said in those long minutes when they'd been alone kept coming to her mind.

"You're not worried they're trying to find a blackmailer this weekend?" she finally ventured.

Carson shouldn't have been surprised.

He'd left Emma alone with Scarlett's actor friend while he spoke to his sister. And Logan probably assumed that Emma already knew about the blackmail note. Still, he hadn't expected to discuss this with anyone outside of the family. Particularly not before his father knew about it.

Briefly, he summed up the events of the last weeks, starting with Scarlett's receipt of the note, to his mother's out-of-character road trip to Yellowstone Park to do some hiking, followed by her fall and coma.

"So Scarlett is going with Logan to find the man who delivered the letter?" Emma asked.

"Logan thought the man looked familiar." Carson didn't trust the actor after what he'd done to Scarlett, but he should have some faith in his sister's judgment. If she trusted him, that had to be good enough.

Even if Carson hated it.

"I'm sorry to ask about it. I know it's none of my business, but ever since Logan used the word blackmail, I've felt uneasy." Emma tried a bite of her dessert, and he realized he'd forgotten all about his.

He picked up his fork and tried to join her in enjoying the last course.

"With good reason. My whole family has been on edge waiting for our private investigator to come up with something." Carson didn't give any details about Paige's mysterious past, since that wasn't his story to share.

Whatever secrets his stepmother was hiding, they were hers to reveal when the time was right. He hadn't asked Scarlett if Logan knew the contents of that note, but maybe he should have.

Either way, the pressure was on to speak to his father as soon as he got back to Cheyenne.

"You were probably looking forward to getting away from those worries tonight," Emma observed. "And then I had to kick the hornet's nest to stir it all up again."

"You didn't know. My family has been a target

for scandalmongers, gold diggers and business rivals in the past. That comes with success." He'd escaped some of that during his years in the rodeo, but successful bull riders were targeted in other ways.

For their fame. By hangers-on who liked the thrill of the sport.

"Still, I'm sorry." She twirled her fork through the merinque. "I've been looking forward to this. Our time together tonight."

His gaze flicked to hers. His unspoken question had somehow been answered, because he knew she was thinking about the same thing as him. His pulse shifted into high gear.

"As have I." He gave up trying to eat any dessert. It was Emma he wanted to taste.

Her lips quirked in the ghost of a nervous smile.

"I—" She set aside her fork. Her elbow bumped against the table slightly, making the candle flames jump inside their tiny hurricane shades. "You should know, I haven't been with anyone since...that whole debacle in my past."

How many years had that been? He couldn't remember, but he knew it had been a long time. He reminded himself to keep that in mind. To take care with her. Of her.

"We can go slowly." He skimmed a touch up her arm, liking the flare of reaction in her eyes as much as the feel of her skin. "You set the pace."

He felt a shiver run through her, the subtle tremble igniting a fierce need of his own.

Emma pivoted on her seat to face him, the thigh-high slit in her skirt giving him a delectable glimpse of her bare leg. "Actually, if I'm being totally honest, three years is sort of feeling like a lifetime right now."

wanted to climb into his lap and kiss him. Wrap herself around him.

"Yes." She forced a jerky nod, her body feeling oddly foreign under the weight of her self-restraint. "I'd like that."

Taking her hand, he drew her to her feet. Her legs tingled with awareness as the cool night breeze fluttered the silk against her skin. There was a scent of applewood in the air from the outdoor hearth.

Carson's warm hand palmed the small of her back, one finger landing on the narrow patch of bare skin between the high-waisted skirt and cropped blouse. Her breasts ached to be touched, the sensitive peaks beading in response to his touch on her back. As he guided her through the French doors and into the living area, she had a vague sense of the cathedral ceiling and a loft area above, the gleaming natural wood walls giving the whole place a dull glow in the dim light from the heavy bronze sconces.

Once he closed the door behind them and stepped briefly into the kitchen to dismiss the wait staff, Carson returned to her side. She let him lead her deeper into the house, past the huge staircase to the hallway that led to the master suite. There, he closed and locked the double doors that separated his quarters from the rest of the home. Emma could see a fire already crackling in the hearth shared on one side by the den and the other side by the bedroom. Carson never hesitated as he drew her left—toward the large bed with a padded leather headboard that rose halfway to the ceiling.

A cream-colored duvet was half pulled back, revealing layers of cream and tan blankets, sheets and a spill of pillows in every size. She only had a moment to take in their surroundings before Carson was there, eye-to-eye with her, his hands cupping her shoulders.

"Are you sure?" He tipped her chin to see her face in the firelight.

She appreciated his concern. Trusted him all the more because of it.

"Completely certain." Dragging in a breath of air tinged with a hint of wood smoke and his aftershave, she felt safe sharing what she wanted. Needed. "I wish tonight would be all about us. A chance to be in the present. Forget about the past."

Understanding lit up his eyes. He curved his palm around her cheek, cradling her face as he stepped closer, narrowing the space between them to the smallest fraction of an inch.

"You can't imagine how much I'm going to like that." His thumb stroked down her cheek.

Once. Twice.

Her lips parted as she leaned into him, sealing her body to his until the only part of them not touching were their lips. She heard his sharp intake of breath and it gratified her to think this attraction affected him as much as it did her.

He threaded his fingers through the hair at the base of her neck. Angled her head for his kiss.

When their lips finally brushed, Emma thought she would come right out of her skin.

Fire blazed over her, flames licking up her legs and roaring over her breasts and belly until she yearned to peel off all her clothes. Feel his bare skin on hers. If Carson knew it—or if he felt that, too—he didn't reveal it with his kiss. He took his time tasting, nipping, exploring. He drew her lower lip between his teeth gently.

Oh. So. Provocatively.

His hands skimmed up her back, fingers gliding over the smooth fabric of her blouse, then venturing beneath it. They stood in the middle of the room and she would have wobbled on her sky-high heels if not for Carson's strong arms around her, keeping her upright. Through the tissue-thin silk of her skirt, she felt his body heat. She couldn't help but roll her hips against his, melting at the feel of him.

She felt more than heard the hungry growl of want that started as a rumble in his chest and ended with a quiet hiss of breath between his teeth as he reared back to look at her. She saw the flare of desire in the molten blue of his eyes and it only edged her own need higher.

"We don't need to rush," he reminded her, his breathing gratifyingly harsh.

"I've waited a long time to feel this way." A lifetime, actually, but she wasn't ready to tell him that. "So I'm finding it hard to wait much more."

She'd never experienced an attraction anywhere close to this. Was it any wonder her hands were a little unsteady as she tugged one end of his bow tie free? Then she smoothed a palm over the hard planes of his chest, very ready to touch all of him.

"In that case—" he reached between them to find the knot on her wrap skirt "—I'd better give you a hand in moving things along."

With barely a flick of his finger, the fabric floated to the floor, leaving her in a tiny pair of bikini panties and very high heels from the waist down.

"It's not fair that I practically fall out of my clothes while yours require so much extra time." She arched an eyebrow at him while she unfastened the top two buttons on his shirt.

"You maneuvered me out of the tie fast enough," he reminded her, flicking open the tiny hook on the neck of her blouse before sliding his hands under the hem.

Seductive sensations chased over her skin, distracting her from the shirt buttons as he cupped her breasts in his palms. She felt the heat of his touch through the lace of her bra, and a shiver rocked her.

"I'm going to be naked in about five more seconds, though. And then I'll be too distracted to get your clothes off." She closed her eyes to better feel all the things he was making her feel.

His thumbs teased circles around the tight peaks through the lace and she was lost. Arching into him, she wondered how much force it might require to tip him back into that huge bed behind him.

Carson kissed his way along her jaw. She clung to him, her fingers wrapping around his arms. Holding tight.

"You let me worry about it," he murmured in her ear, pausing briefly before his lips continued down her neck. Nipping, licking, driving her mad.

"Carson." She breathed his name like a plea, unsure what she wanted.

Him, obviously.

But all of him felt so good, she couldn't decide where to touch next. And all of *her* felt so damn good, she couldn't get enough of his touch. His body. His *mouth*, which drove the hunger higher with each movement of his lips.

He wrapped his arms around her then, lifted her high against his chest and deposited her in the middle of his bed. She tried to keep him there with her, but he edged back to stand at the foot of it.

With deliberate fingers, he unfastened the buttons on his tuxedo shirt, one after the other, his blue gaze never leaving hers.

Intrigued by the hint of muscle in the gaping V of the placket, she lifted herself up on her arms to better admire him.

When he shouldered out of his jacket, the shirt

went with it, giving her a view of his squared shoulders and strong arms. Inspired, she took the hem of her wrinkled blouse and lifted it over her head, letting the material fall along the side of the bed while Carson's hands moved to his belt. And his zipper.

Firelight bathed his skin in a tawny glow while leaving his face in shadow. She watched, fascinated by the movement of his abs as he stepped out of the trousers. Then she stared at the boxers beneath them. She forgot all about her own undressing, her fingers going still on the bra straps she'd been about to shrug out of.

Carson was…impressive.

All of him.

"I. Um." Her throat was dry. She'd forgotten about birth control. Still, she couldn't quite link her thoughts to her speech. She was too busy ogling.

A hint of a grin played at his lips. "That's exactly how I'm feeling right now," he told her as he joined her on the bed, stretching out beside her.

His thigh was hot next to hers, the bristle of his hair tickling her oversensitive skin.

She watched as he turned her toward him, flicking open the hooks of her bra so the lace fell aside. He kissed each peak, making her forget everything but this. Him.

The want.

"So beautiful." He said the words into her skin,

pressing them in with kisses as he worked his way up her chest.

When he reached the hollow of her throat where the diamond horseshoe pendant lay, he kissed beneath it, the stones clinking dully on his teeth.

She wrapped an arm around him, pulling herself closer to him while he covered her hip with one hand. He spanned her belly with his palm and desire pooled between her thighs. He slid the lace panties down and off. She was so very ready.

Except that she hadn't brought any protection.

"Do you have anything?" she blurted, placing a hand on his chest, needing to settle this now before she got so caught up she forgot everything else. "I mean, do you have—"

He reached behind her head on the bed and came back with a foil packet.

"I smuggled one in my jacket pocket. Just in case."

"One?" She couldn't hide the hint of dismay.

"There are more in a bathroom somewhere," he promised, tearing open the condom and rolling it into place.

"Good." Relief settled over her, allowing her to be more fully in the moment. To soak up the pleasure of being with him. "That's very good."

Their eyes locked. Emma reached to touch his jaw. She kissed him, her hips sidling closer to his. Grazing the hard length of him.

He slid an arm around her and rolled her onto her

back before he settled himself between her thighs. She felt her heartbeat quicken for the space of a few beats.

And then, he eased inside her by slow degrees, taking his time and kissing her. She buried her face in his neck, breathing in the scent of him and tasting the hint of salt on his skin. Pleasure built as he thrust deeper.

Wordless, she could only hold on while he coaxed responses from her body that surprised her. Release came fast and hard, her body clenching around his in one lush spasm after another. He went very still, waiting, wringing every bit of delicious sensation from her body as he kissed her breasts, drawing her deep into his mouth.

And then, while she was still breathless, he began to thrust inside her all over again. Slowly at first. But then building momentum. This time, he touched the damp heat between her thighs, close to where their bodies joined, and she flew apart on contact. She writhed with another toe-curling release. Except this time, Carson came with her, his body tensing everywhere, sweat popping out along his shoulders where she held on to him.

Heat broke over her again and again. She heard his hoarse shout, but her heart pounded so loudly in her own ears, the sound only vibrated through her. He was careful afterward not to collapse on her; instead, he fell heavily on his side and turned her with him, holding her so close that her temple rested just above his heart. Her eyelids fluttered shut, and she settled deeper into him, her own heart finally slowing down along with her breathing.

Sleep could have claimed her if not for the slow return of reason. As happy as it made her to think she'd fully reclaimed her life now, moving on from her painful past in every way, Emma recognized that this night would change things between them. Irrevocably.

She tried to quiet those thoughts while Carson pulled a sheet around them, tucking her close. But too soon, the questions bubbled to the surface. Would he regret what they'd shared? Was he in a hurry to rejoin his family while the McNeills tried to find their blackmailer?

He'd been vague about the details of the note, and she certainly understood why. But the fact that he hadn't shared much with her about all the tumultuous events in his world spoke volumes about her place in his life. Had she acted too rashly? It had seemed so logical an hour ago, and now as her body cooled, she wasn't as sure.

"Emma?" Carson's voice, soft and close to her ear, startled her eyes open. "Everything okay? You were frowning."

He tucked a finger into the chain on her necklace and straightened the pendant. The cool platinum slid smoothly against her skin.

"Yes. I just—" Hesitating, she weighed how much to say about what was on her mind. "I feel a bit guilty keeping you here now that I know all you have going on back home."

"I wanted to bring you here," he assured her, levering up on one elbow, his forehead furrowed. "That was my choice."

"But that was before you knew your sister was going out of town." She didn't mean to stir trouble. She also didn't want to be taken by surprise if Carson decided he wanted to leave.

And maybe a part of her recognized that what she'd shared with Carson gave him far more power to hurt her than Austin ever had.

"I don't understand." Carson tensed as he straightened. "What are you saying?"

She drew the sheet tighter to her chest, knowing it would be easier on her if she was the one who set boundaries. Who made sure her heart was safe. "I'm saying we should consider flying home tonight."

Carson didn't argue.

Not even a blind man could miss the walls Emma put up after they made love. As much as he was tempted to kiss her and entice her to stay, he knew that would simply delay the inevitable. She was having second thoughts, and he knew she'd been through a lot. He'd make a tactical retreat. For now.

That was why, shortly after midnight, Carson

found himself back in Cheyenne. He walked up the flagstone path to the main doors of the Creek Spill ranch house, Emma by his side. She had fallen asleep on the short plane ride home. Or pretended to. He honestly wasn't sure. He simply understood Emma needed to retreat. And after the way their night together had rocked him, too, maybe that wasn't such a bad idea. When he'd pursued the attraction full tilt, he had anticipated the off-the-charts sensuality of their joining. But he sure as hell hadn't expected the lingering need to protect Emma. Keep her safe.

That element of his relationship with her—wanting to take care of her—complicated things. Hell, here he was, protecting her from *him*.

Pausing to disarm the security system, Carson opened the door for her. He'd given her one of his T-shirts for the ride home. She wore it with her long skirt, the neck of the shirt sliding off one of her shoulders. He wanted her even more now. Even knowing that she was pulling away. Even when he understood their time together could be limited.

But for tonight, he would let her go.

Tomorrow, he'd figure out his next move.

"I understand if you need to leave," Emma told him as she slipped off her high heels and bent to pick them up. The brief glimpse of her thigh through the slit of that long skirt threatened to shake his restraint. "If you want to be with your family. I feel totally safe here."

She was giving him the green light to leave. Another push for space? Frustration ate at him as he flipped on the elk horn chandelier over the main staircase. He had to remind himself they were both tired.

"It's late. I hadn't planned on leaving." Although he had promised his sister he'd speak to their father as soon as he returned to Cheyenne. "And I would appreciate it if this information about a blackmailer targeting the McNeills remains strictly between us."

"Of course." She halted on the first step, turning to look back at him as he pulled two bottles of water from a drawer in the refrigerator. "I would never share something like that."

He nodded, trusting her word on that. Rejoining her on the stairs, he handed her a bottle of water.

"Thank you." He would head to his parents' home on the Black Creek Ranch first thing in the morning. "Not everyone in my family is aware of what's happening yet." A scandal had the power to affect far more people than just his brothers and half sisters. There were McNeill cousins all over the world.

His phone vibrated in the pocket of his tux jacket, which he was carrying over one arm.

"I'll let you take that," Emma told him as they reached the top of the stairs. "Thank you for a beautiful evening, Carson."

He could see her retreating and felt the sting of

disappointment, though he knew he needed to give her space.

He kissed her cheek and stroked a thumb along her jaw, just enough to hear the gratifying intake of breath. See the way her pupils dilated a fraction. When he backed away, though, she hurried into her room and shut the door.

It was a fitting end to a night when he felt like he'd made one misstep after another with her. Withdrawing his phone, he checked his messages. The text from his dad caught his eye.

Paige in tears. Says she won't rest until Ventura is off McNeill property. Need help calming her down.

Carson didn't think twice.

Tossing his tuxedo jacket on a chair in the hall, he headed back down the stairs and out the door. Rearming the security system, he jumped in his truck to see what he could do. Because Donovan McNeill never asked for help. If he admitted that he needed it now, with his own wife, something was really wrong.

And it gave Carson an uneasy feeling that his stepmother was upset about Antonio Ventura being in town. Hadn't Emma just mentioned that family tonight over dinner? She said her mother had compared the Venturas to the McNeills.

It was probably just a coincidence.

But he couldn't ignore his family when they needed him now more than ever. Carson planned to look more carefully into the *Winning the West* director to figure out why having him around would upset his stepmother so much.

Even if that meant the next step in Carson's pursuit of his stuntwoman guest would have to wait.

Nine

Alone in her suite, Emma stepped out of the steamy shower and toweled off with one of the Turkish terry cloth bath sheets. She should be exhausted from the long day and the stress leading up to the stunt, all the wondering if she would be able to pull it off.

But her evening with Carson had left her wound up. Exhilarated. She was unable to settle down even though it was well after midnight. Their time together had been surreal, so special it almost felt like it had happened to another person.

But now she wasn't sure how to face the days ahead with him when she knew that what seemed life-changing for her was just a passing pleasure for someone like Carson McNeill. That had been the point of her mother's urgent texts earlier today. A warning to Emma not to fall for a McNeill the way Jane Layton had once fallen for her employer, Emilio Ventura, father of the man now directing *Winning the West.* The affair had destroyed Jane's marriage, probably playing a role in Emma's father's suicide, although Jane had never admitted as much. Hurt stabbed through Emma at the thought of her dad, her memories of him painfully scant.

She combed the tangles from her damp hair, wishing she could sort through her muddled thoughts as easily.

She recognized how she might be following in her mother's unwise footsteps. Because while neither Carson nor Emma was married to other people, there was still the same kind of imbalance between them. Carson moved in a world of privilege and wealth that allowed him to jet around the country at a moment's notice. Emma was a maid's daughter still trying to duck a jailbird ex. What was more, she wasn't sure she'd come to terms with the fact that she'd stayed in a relationship with Austin after he'd hit her the first time. She wanted to think she would have kicked him to the curb on her own without the intervention of people at her gym the day he'd been arrested. But that decision had been taken out of her hands by the courts, so she'd never had the satisfaction of making it herself.

All this time—training harder, becoming a stuntwoman, getting physically stronger—and she still had no idea if she was tougher where it counted. Emotionally.

That fear was what had sent her running from the best night of her life. The best man she'd ever met.

Yet she had his T-shirt to remember what had transpired between them. Slipping it back on now over her naked body still warm from the shower, Emma padded to the bed and slid between the covers. Everything about her room was luxurious, from the high thread count sheets and white goose down duvet to the thick pile rugs and custom furnishings with rustic touches. Yet the thing she liked most about it was wearing Carson's shirt. The soft gray cotton held the clean scent of detergent, but underneath that, just barely, she could catch the scent of him. His aftershave. His soap and skin.

She switched off the lamp on the table beside the bed, but the skylight overhead kept the room from being totally dark. She closed her eyes, knowing she'd dream of Carson. Only to have her phone chime with a text.

My sister Scarlett asked me for your #. She has a question about the Ventura family. Do you mind if I share? I'm at my father's now. My stepmother is not well.

Emma bit her lip, hurting for Carson. He must be worried about his stepmom. She wished she could offer him some comfort. But why did Scarlett want to speak to *her*? Surely Logan King knew more about Antonio Ventura than she did. Although, when Logan had asked Emma about her riding, she had mentioned her early lessons at the Ventura family's stables. Maybe he'd shared that information with Carson's sister.

But Logan King had worked with Antonio on a film abroad. She remembered reading about it in the Hollywood tabloids. Her mother's apartment was always full of them, her conversations dotted with references to film and television personalities—especially the ones who stopped by the Ventura residence while Jane was working.

Emma had always thought it peculiar that her mother would choose to continue in the employ of a man who'd once been her lover. A man who'd broken her heart. Emma's counselor had suggested maybe it was a way for Jane to remain close to him. To feel like she was a part of his life.

Remembering that made Emma breathe a bit easier about her night with Carson, at least. She'd moved on from Austin—completely. Being with Carson tonight had proven that.

Taking a deep breath, she texted Carson back.

Of course Scarlett can have my number. Is there anything I can do to help with your stepmother? I'm sorry to hear she's not improving.

She waited a moment, wondering how she could help. But he responded quickly.

No, but thank you. Rest up from your big day. Hours on horseback can be tiring when you're not used to it. I'll check in with you in the morning.

He was a thoughtful, good man to think of her comfort when his own family was dealing with so much. It would be easy to fall for him.

Lying back down on the bed, Emma tried not to think about that. About how incredible the night had been. Instead, she deleted all of her mother's messages, refusing to get caught up in them. She scheduled a message to go out at nine o'clock in the morning, to avoid an all-night text fest with her mother, who often had trouble sleeping. Emma wrote a few sentences about how much she loved the job and how beautiful the scenery was in Wyoming. She ended with a quick line of assurance she'd visit when she returned home.

Done.

She wondered if she'd hear from Scarlett tonight. It gave Emma an uneasy feeling to know that Scarlett had gone to LA to look for a blackmailer and suddenly had questions about the family that had been a part of Emma's life for as long as she could remember. A shadowy part, yes. But she'd spent time in the Ventura home, occasionally helping her mother clean. Emma had taken those long-ago riding lessons at their stables, in fact.

Now, closing her eyes once again, Emma breathed deeply to catch the scent of Carson in his T-shirt. She tucked her nose into the ribbed neckline, rubbing her cheek along the seam, remembering his touch. But the sweet dreams of what they'd shared seemed out of reach with a new fear creeping closer.

What if she never experienced another night like this one? Never felt a touch to rival Carson McNeill's? Because if that was true—and she feared it could be—maybe she couldn't afford to waste the rest of her time in Cheyenne being scared of what he made her feel.

Scarlett was alone with Logan for the first time since they'd touched down in LA.

No doubt she was a little nervous about that, but that was only part of the reason she was texting her brother for the twentieth time to try to get an update on what was going on back home. Yes, she was trying to distract herself from the prospect of being in Logan's Malibu home for the night. But also, how could Carson be so stingy with details?

She sat in a bright turquoise chair in the midcentury modern living room at Logan's place on the beach, the long fireplace beside her taking the chill out of the air from the breeze blowing off the Pacific. The whole living space opened onto an outdoor patio, with what must be stunning views of the water during the daytime. But now, well after midnight, she only had the salty scent of the air and a few boats bobbing off shore to clue her in to the massive ocean crashing on the rocks below.

"Let's go sit outside," Logan urged her for the second time, his fingers grazing her arm lightly as he stood near her chair. He'd been the consummate gentleman all evening, taking her to one of the best restaurants in the city for dinner and then making good on his promise to find the guy who gave her the blackmail note.

Except the mystery man had apparently skipped town, according to Logan's bartender source at the club where it had all gone down. But they'd learned his name was Ron and he used to work as a groom for the Ventura family stables.

Or so he claimed. No one had seen him around the club in the last week, and the bartender had overheard the guy tell someone else at the bar that he was going to Belize. All of which Scarlett had texted to Carson. In return, he let her know he'd already broken the news about her mother's blackmailer to their father.

"I just want to get a few more answers from my brother." Scarlett was already texting as fast as her fingers would allow, her skin still humming pleasantly from Logan's brief touch. Would she be able to resist the attraction? Did she even want to? She hadn't thought it through, and wasn't sure she trusted her decision-making power now that the man was so temptingly close. Clearing her throat, she paused and glanced up at her host for the weekend. "Carson said he told Dad about—"

Breaking off, she remembered she hadn't told Logan the contents of the blackmail note. He'd asked, but hadn't pushed her to reveal details. And since she wasn't sure how much to trust him, she'd been vague.

"It's okay," Logan assured her, his fingers brushing along her shoulder in a gesture meant to comfort. "You don't have to share specifics. But you've put a lot of time into helping your family for the night. You deserve to relax." His green eyes locked on her, making her stomach flip. "Come outside with me for a minute. Unwind before bed."

Her heart skipped a beat.

Logan had worn a gray suit tonight for dinner, but his jacket had disappeared along with his tie. Those two open buttons on his custom-tailored dress shirt didn't show off much of him. And yet…to Scarlett's eyes, he appeared appealingly undone.

She nodded, leaving her phone on the chair so she wouldn't be tempted to keep checking for another of Carson's terse one-liners that told her nothing.

"You may be the first person in my life who has ever implied there's such a thing as 'enough' time to give to my family." Scarlett smoothed nervous fingers down her pink skirt embroidered with exotic birds. The green one-shouldered blouse she wore with it fluttered against her skin as they left the shelter of the living area and stepped out onto the stone patio.

Logan's hand palmed the small of her back lightly to guide her toward the two big seats positioned to look out over the rocks that led to the beach. Landscape lighting illuminated the path.

She dropped into one of the cushioned Adirondack chairs. How had she become the focus of this man's attention when he had his pick of the world's most beautiful women? Scarlett wouldn't even register in her own very attractive family if not for the glittery accessories and flashy clothing choices. Whatever it was he saw in her, he had the most flattering way of conveying his interest with his eyes. How they'd followed her all night.

"I spent my whole childhood scrambling to help my own family stay afloat." He settled into the chair beside hers, resting his arms on the wide wooden armrests. "Only to have things fall apart in a spectacular way." Giving her a sidelong glance, he shook his head. "Not that my criminal relations are anything like the McNeills. But I did learn the need to carve out goals that were mine alone."

She tipped her face to feel the light mist of ocean spray borne on the wind, wondering what it must be like for Logan to live in this dream home now after being on the run and sometimes homeless with his family.

"I'm going to do that. Follow my own goals, I mean." She'd crunched the numbers to prove to her father she'd more than repaid the family for financing her education through the years she'd worked as an assistant to the Black Creek Ranch foreman. "I'm giving my two-week notice at the end of the summer. Then I hope I'll be able to move in with my friend Lucie who already lives here." Lucie had relocated to LA from London last year and worked in casting.

Maybe it was too late for Scarlett to pursue her own dream of acting. But she'd never know if she didn't try.

"Good for you." Logan's hand slid closer to where hers rested on her armrest. "And you are welcome to stay here anytime if things don't work out with your friend. It can be hard to find a place."

Surprised by his offer, she turned to gauge his expression and see if he was serious. "You don't think it would be awkward for you to have an old fling sleeping upstairs when you brought home a hot date?"

"I've been angling hard for you to be my hot date as often as possible." He sat forward in his seat, swiveling toward her. "But perhaps I need to be clearer about what I want." He didn't touch her except where his pinky finger stroked along the top of hers on the armrest.

Just there.

She wasn't sure if it was that simple touch or his words that sent heat licking all over her skin.

"I—" Her voice cracked. She took another breath and reminded herself that this man had vanished from her life without a word. "You have a funny way of showing it."

"So you keep saying. And if you won't accept my apology and my assurance that it was a mistake, I'm going to ask for a do-over." He curled his pinky around hers, holding it there. "I want a chance to make things right with you. I had hoped this weekend would be a start—by helping you find that guy who passed you the note."

She stared into those green eyes for a long moment while one wave after another broke on the shore below, a soothing sound that lulled her to acquiesce. To wish that what she'd felt with him that one night together hadn't been a mistake. The heat in his gaze mirrored everything she was feeling.

"I appreciate that." She knew it was only a matter of time before Carson's PI figured out who was harassing her family, and discovering some clues to the identity of the man who'd delivered the threatening message was going to speed things along. "But I have only myself to blame if I make the same mistake twice."

The muscle in his jaw flexed. He nodded, rising to his feet.

"I understand. In that case, I'll let you get to bed.

I know you must be tired." He offered her his hand and she took it, allowing him to help her to her feet.

Regret nipped at her that they hadn't been able to put the past behind them. That she'd clung to evidence of his treachery even though he'd apologized. And explained.

Was she being petty? Overindulging wounded pride?

As she walked with him into the living area, she second-guessed herself.

"Don't forget your phone." Logan leaned over the chair where she'd left it earlier and passed the device to her.

She didn't bother checking it, too worried she might be screwing up the possibility of an incredible relationship with a man who'd done everything he could to make things right between them.

He shut down a few of the lights on a post near the stairs and then hit a button to close the living area doors, locking out the sound of the waves for the night.

Scarlett bit her lip as she followed him up the stairs toward the bedrooms, her chance at salvaging this night fading.

As they reached the landing, Scarlett stepped in front of him. Placed a hand on his warm chest.

"Logan?" Nerves trembled through her. But damn it, she didn't want to lose this chance if she'd been wrong about him.

"Scarlett." There was a weary note in his tone, a wariness in his gaze. "Honey, if you're not ready for more, I think we need to retreat and regroup." Gently, he bracketed her shoulders.

And shuffled her aside.

But that was because he was being gentlemanly, right? She reminded herself she was supposed to be carving out goals of her own, damn it.

And she wanted this. Him.

"Consider the hatchet buried." She stepped in front of him again. Determined. "Also, that the do-over has been granted. And that I'm ready for more."

She felt a piece of her wounded heart heal at the way his nostrils flared and his pupils dilated a fraction, the irises becoming a narrow strip of color around the dark centers.

For a moment, however, he said nothing. He merely stared back at her, breathing hard in the narrow hallway full of bright artwork and tiny spotlights.

Then, before she could restate her case, Logan stepped toward her. His hands skimmed her waist as his lips closed on hers. He lifted her up, bringing her eye level to kiss her thoroughly, his strong arms banding her to him.

Just when she'd gone breathless, her thoughts scattering and disappearing, Logan broke the kiss. He leaned back to take her measure, her body melting into his.

"You're not going to regret it," he assured her, his voice a hot vibration against her ear as he opened the door to a bedroom. "Not for a second. Not ever."

She ignored the warning voice inside that reminded her that was what she'd hoped the first time. Because if Scarlett ever wanted to start over—to reinvent her life and sense of purpose—she wasn't going to second-guess herself anymore.

Ten

Carson urged his mount forward through a thicket, determined to find Emma after his long night spent at his father's house. Tracking down his houseguest wasn't as simple as joining her for breakfast in the kitchen, however. His housekeeper had told him Emma went to the stables. One of the grooms had shown him the general direction she'd ridden.

But in the end, Carson had needed to text Dax to pinpoint her exact location.

Now, with afternoon approaching and the sun disappearing behind the storm clouds moving in, Carson finally saw her with his own eyes as he broke through the tree line. In the distance, a slim figure in black running shorts and a tank top sprinted up a hillside, arms pumping as her hair bounced in a topknot on her head.

The sight of her there, working with a relentlessness apparent even from this distance, hammered home to him how driven she was.

Or, perhaps, how deeply wounded.

As much as he wanted to believe that Emma's workouts were a way for her to stay on top of her profession, a part of him wondered if it was more a need to prove her physical strength. Did old fears spur her to be stronger just in case she needed to protect herself again? Catching sight of her bodyguard off to one side of the meadow, Carson waved him off, releasing Dax from his protective duty now that Carson had found her.

A nudge to his horse's flanks set the bay mare in motion again, faster this time. The animal seemed as eager as Carson for the burst of speed after the tedious pace of searching for the past half hour. Yet Carson's need to reach Emma's side was deeper, memories from their night together never far from his mind. He'd wanted to give her space after the way she'd backed off. With their time together so damn brief, however, he found it impossible to stay away today. Especially with a thunderstorm due soon. Did she even realize it was turning darker by the minute?

By the time Carson reached the base of the hillside, Emma was running down it, her long strides fluid and athletic. She must have noticed him, but her focus remained on the path until she slowed down. Then her gaze went right to him, the expression in her brown eyes concerned.

"How is your stepmother?" Emma walked in a slow circle, stretching her legs with an occasional lunge. "Is she showing any sign of improvement?"

Carson swung down from the mare, the need to be closer to Emma drawing him. He dropped the reins to ground tie the animal.

"Not unless you count the fact that her sedative finally kicked in around seven o'clock this morning." The time with his father and Paige had been agonizing. "I left so my dad could get some sleep while my stepmom was resting. She's got a health aide with her for the day, so I'll be getting updates."

Emma stopped in front of him, her forehead damp from her workout, her breathing still fast. A pang of empathy gripped him hard. No woman should have to run from the kind of demons that haunted her. He had to battle the urge to pull her against him and assure her he'd never let anything happen to her again.

"What about you?" she asked, her brown eyes tracking his. Her hands fluttered close to his chest, as if she wasn't sure about touching him. Then, thankfully, they landed there. "Did you get any sleep?"

A warning rumble of thunder sounded in the distance.

"Enough." He didn't want her to worry, and he had too much on his mind to close his eyes for long. He took her hands in his and lifted them to his mouth, kissing the back of one, then the other. "And it's not me who was supposed to take it easy today," he chided gently. "I can't imagine what your legs feel like after the hours in the saddle the last few days. Especially when you haven't ridden in years. No amount of exercise can really prepare you for that."

A sudden breeze whipped the wisps of hair that had slid free from her topknot.

"I was sore," she admitted. "That was half the reason I thought I'd come out here and run. To loosen up."

He wanted to get her out of the weather before the storm broke, but something about what she'd said caught his attention. He released her hands to stroke back a glossy lock of her chestnut-colored hair. "Half the reason?"

"I was also trying to gain some perspective on what happened between us yesterday. And how I felt about that."

His mare whinnied anxiously as the sky darkened, a far-off crack of lightning flickering in the mountains.

But Carson remained rooted to the spot, hating that he'd given Emma any cause for regret. "Emma, my whole life I've been the reckless one in my family. But with you, I swear I tried my best to be careful. To go slow."

"And you were careful. Absolutely." She fidgeted,

freeing the knot in her hair, letting the wavy mass blow in the wind while slipping the pink band around her wrist like a bracelet. "I was the one who rushed things, so that's on me." She peered up at the sky as another clap of thunder sounded. "And it's pretty clear that *I'm* the reckless one, since I didn't even look at the weather before I jogged out here."

Carson followed her gaze. "We won't make it back to the main house before the skies open up. But my brother's place is just over that ridge." He remembered how eager Brock had been to escape the filmmaking for the weekend. Picking up the bay mare's reins, Carson swung up on her back. "You can ride with me."

He held out a hand to her, fat raindrops beginning to fall.

"Are you sure?" She chewed her lip nervously.

"Hurry," he urged, feeling the horse's agitation. He nudged the stirrup forward with his boot. "Use the stirrup."

Emma stepped up and he shifted forward in the saddle, giving her room behind him so he could keep better control of the mare. By the time Emma was settled, her arms around his waist, the rain had let loose.

The bay needed no urging. At Carson's command, the quarter horse took off, hooves pounding, long legs stretching out into a gallop. Carson leaned forward and Emma did the same, her cheek and chest warm against his back while the downpour turned cold.

The path to Brock's place was well-worn. He'd recently completed his house after years of picking away at it in his free time. It sat right on the Black Creek, the center point between his brothers' ranches, so he had easy access to both without having to commit to either. When Brock had lobbied for this slice of land from their father, Carson never imagined his quiet, almost taciturn younger brother would build something so damn beautiful with his own two hands.

The bay would have headed for the stables if not for Carson tugging her toward the house. He wanted to drop off Emma under the cover of a deep vaulted porch first. Once she was under the shelter of the overhang, he took the bay into the stables, grateful to find a ranch hand at work. The younger man seemed pleased to escape the job of stall mucking for a little while to brush out the bay, allowing Carson to sprint back to where Emma waited. Her wet clothes clung to curves that had him aching to touch her again.

He entered the last code he remembered for the front door. It wasn't armed with a security system, but Brock had used a keyless entry. Thankfully, the lock gave and the handle turned.

"Oh, thank goodness," Emma gasped as they stepped inside, dripping water all over the mat.

"I'll get us some towels." Toeing off his boots and removing his hat, Carson padded across the tile floor through the kitchen to the laundry room. A stack of folded white towels sat in a basket on the dryer.

When he returned to the foyer, Emma had her running sneakers off. Rivulets still streamed down her bare shoulders from her wet hair, her cotton workout clothes shrink-wrapping her body in a way that made him forget all about the chill from the rain.

"Thank goodness," she said again. Her teeth were chattering as she reached for a towel. "I can't believe how cold the rain felt."

"When the weather comes down off the mountains it's like that." He tore his eyes away from her, knowing he needed to back off after what she'd said about rushing into things.

But then a good idea occurred to him as he patted his own towel over his face.

"Come with me." He took her hand, leading her into the living room.

"I'm all wet," she protested. "We're leaving footprints everywhere."

When he reached the doors to the deck, he pointed to the sunken tub tucked under another vaulted porch. Steam escaped the leather cover in every direction. His brother must have the heater on a timer.

Bless him.

"Since we're wet already, we could always warm up in there." He pointed to the hot tub, but Emma was already darting past him to get outside.

She'd given zero consideration to what she was wearing, not caring if the shorts and tank went in the hot tub since she was drenched already.

And chilled.

So when Carson lifted half of the leather cover from the tub, which emitting a cloud of steam over her, she simply stepped down into the bubbles. She found a molded seat in one corner and dropped into it so the hot water reached her neck.

"This feels amazing." Closing her eyes, she leaned back against the neck pillow as her body thawed.

The tub was recessed under the overhang of the vaulted porch so the rain didn't reach them, but she could see out over the landscaped yard to the wide creek that rushed past the house. River stone lined the bank of the creek and it had been used generously around the house, too. The bottom half of the house was stone—or at least faced with the gray rock—while the upper portion was natural wood. It was both rustic and luxurious, with deep porches to enjoy the incredible Wyoming vistas.

She pulled in a breath, her body relaxing as she warmed up, and glanced over at Carson.

And promptly swallowed her tongue.

He, apparently, had no intention of getting into the tub with his clothes on. His jeans long gone, he stood on the deck in fitted black boxer shorts that hugged his muscular thighs. He hauled his wet T-shirt up and off, flinging it to the planked floor before he stepped down into the tub alongside her.

She didn't blink, unwilling to miss a moment of Carson McNeill. The night before had been so heated and, thanks to her, too rushed. She hadn't really gotten to enjoy seeing him like this—unfiltered and utterly masculine in the light of day.

As he sank into the seat next to her—close to her, so his body grazed hers at her elbow and knee—she felt a wave of hot desire that had nothing to do with the temperature of the tub.

Hadn't she thought to herself last night that she should take advantage of this week? This time with him that was a surreal pleasure she'd never be able to replicate?

"Are—um—we alone?" Her voice was too husky with want to sound as cool and casual as she would have liked.

No doubt he guessed what she was really wondering.

He turned blue eyes on her, an answering desire evident there.

"There's a ranch hand in the stables, but the house is very much empty." His focus dipped to her mouth and hunger for him swelled.

"Whose house is this?" She licked her lips, remembering his kiss and how it felt. How he tasted.

"My brother Brock lives here, but I texted with him this morning and he was still in Bakersfield, California, where he plans to spend the night."

"Does he have a maid?" Emma knew her mother had walked in on people in compromising situations during her years in service to the Ventura family. She wouldn't want to make things awkward for Carson by being careless. "Or domestic staff?"

Just outside the deep overhang of the porch roofline, the rain pounded harder, torrents of water falling in sheets.

"Brock cares more about his horses than anything else, so he only hires help for them. He doesn't have anyone for the house." Carson angled toward her, his shoulders rising above the water line. "We are absolutely, one hundred percent alone."

Her belly flipped. The possibility of being with him again became real. A breath-stealing proposition.

Steam rose from his skin, framing all that taut muscle in soft focus. She ran a hand over his upper arm to feel his tantalizing strength. He sucked in a breath. A deep thrill coursed through her to know she affected him that way.

"How fortunate," she murmured, tracing a droplet of water with her finger as it slid from his shoulder down his chest.

She thought about licking the next one. Chasing a drop with her tongue.

"Is it?" He studied her, his expression guarded. "Last night, I got the idea you weren't ready to spend more time alone with me."

She smoothed her palm on his skin, flattening it against him. She wanted to press all the rest of herself to him just that same way.

"I've since reconsidered." She ventured forward, needing to close the distance between them, wanting to show him she was thoroughly invested in this. In him. "I'm living in the moment from now on. No more borrowing trouble. No more fearing what tomorrow brings."

When her lips hovered near his, she breathed him in, anticipating what was to come. She took her time in a way she hadn't last night.

She kissed him, knowing that he was letting her make the first move because of how she'd retreated the day before. And she appreciated that. Respected the kind of man who did things that way.

At first, she was the one who gave the kiss. It was a tentative brush of exploration. A makeup kiss for the way she'd pulled back the day before.

But Carson had another kind of kiss in mind. He lifted a hand to her cheek, tilted her face and angled his jaw. Just like that, the contact went from tentative to provocative.

Sweet to sensual.

Flames streaked through her. It was as if they'd never touched before, as if it was all new. Longing and need swirled between them. Carson shifted closer, one thigh settling between hers, fanning the fire. Making her restless with want.

She wished she wasn't wearing her running shorts. That she could press against him and he could be inside her already.

Now.

But he just kissed her. Exploring her thoroughly, making her feel like she'd never been kissed until now. Until this. The sensation made her all the more desperate to make this moment with him count. To soak in the feel of him, the taste and scent and magic of what they did to one another.

Then he pulled back and she felt dazed. Unfocused.

"Come on." He took her hand, tugging her upward.

She followed blindly, water sluicing off their bodies as they stepped out into the cool, storm-laden air. He didn't lead her toward the main house, however. Instead, he headed to a small wooden shed she hadn't noticed off to one side of the deck. There were no windows on the building, and as Carson pulled open the door, steam wafted out along with dull red light.

A sauna.

She followed him inside, and he closed the door and locked it behind them. Her heartbeat went wild. He stepped toward her, casting a strong, impressive shadow in the dim room. To hell with the possibility of regrets. She needed him. Now.

Before he could take a second step, she flung herself into his arms.

Eleven

It had been less than twenty-four hours since he'd slept with Emma, but it felt like they'd been apart for a lifetime.

He tossed his jeans on a bench before he hauled her closer, lifting her up in his arms to take her mouth with his. Over and over again. The hunger for her hadn't been sated yesterday. If anything, last night had stirred a deeper longing unlike anything he'd ever felt. He speared a hand into her damp hair, losing himself in the slick mating of mouths.

The dry heat of the sauna turned steamy from their bodies and wet clothes. Clothes he needed gone. He peeled her shirt away, breaking the kiss just long enough to tug the clinging sports fabric up and off.

It left her breasts bared and impossible to resist, the rosy peaks tightening under his tongue as he tasted each one.

He toed open an insulated box under one bench seat and bent to retrieve fresh towels from the storage bin, tossing them on one wide bench beside the sopping jeans he'd brought with him since there was a condom in one pocket.

Her hands were already busy gliding down his back, smoothing over his hips, reaching beneath his boxers to stroke him. He bit off an oath, teeth grinding at the need for restraint. It was worth it, though, when she glanced up at him with her wide dark eyes full of surprise at what she did to him so damned effortlessly.

He peeled off her shorts and panties and she dragged his boxers down. He fumbled for the jeans' pocket on the bench behind him, but before he'd found it, she was wrapping her calf around his, bringing all that sweet feminine warmth closer to where he wanted her. Needed her.

Dropping to sit on the bench, he found the condom as she straddled him, her legs sliding around his waist in a way that pushed him to the brink. And he wasn't even inside her yet.

Emma took the foil packet from him, tearing it open and rolling the condom into place.

Then, finally, he was thrusting deep inside her.

At last.

His forehead tipped to hers as he guided her hips, steadied her on top of him. The perfection of the moment, of her, slammed home, making him want to hold on to this for as long as he could. When he moved inside her, her moan echoed his, reminding him he wasn't alone in this. She was right there with him, feeling all the pleasure in this union that he did, going through every breathless sensation.

He didn't want to ever let her go.

The thought hit with all the force of a release, but it was hers that came first, sending her body into one lush spasm after another. Seeing her that way, unguarded and undone, made him forget everything else. He could only hold on to her hips and steady himself as she moved. When he followed her a moment later, finding a level of completion he hadn't experienced with anyone else, Carson hugged her tightly. His arms around her neck, her legs around his waist, they clung to each other like there was nothing else in the world. And they stayed like that long afterward.

But as their breathing finally slowed and awareness returned, Carson knew he was playing with fire to keep seeing Emma. To be with her this way and want more.

Closing his eyes, he allowed his head to rest on the wall behind him, thinking it would be easier if he didn't care so much. For years, he'd had easy relationships because they were safe. Neat.

No one got hurt.

His sister Maisie hadn't been all that wrong when she'd told him he only dated people he wouldn't fall for. People he wouldn't marry. Losing his mother as a kid would have been difficult enough, but watching helplessly as she was trampled by a bull had provided enough loss and heartbreak for a lifetime. Carson wasn't against relationships. Just the deep, profound ones that could level maximum damage.

Being the reckless twin had served him well in that regard, keeping people at arm's length.

Yet now, with the most desirable, fascinating woman he'd ever met raining lazy kisses along his shoulder, Carson recognized he was in danger of getting too close. Caring too deeply.

Worse? Maybe he already did.

An hour later, Emma dressed in her freshly dried clothes in a downstairs bathroom at Brock McNeill's house.

Carson had run their things on a high heat cycle to dry quickly after their time in the sauna. He had been thoughtful, laying out deli meats, cheeses and fresh bread for sandwiches while they waited for the laundry to finish. He'd entertained her with stories about his absent brother, recalling some tales from their bull riding days before Brock had left the sport.

But something about Carson's manner seemed… off.

Not distant, really. She couldn't call him that since

he'd been perfectly charming. Yet she sensed a new barrier between them that hadn't been there before. Like he'd been the one to pull away this time, only he did a much better job of disguising it than she had last night.

Or was she looking for trouble where there was none?

"Ready?" Carson asked as she emerged from the bathroom. He was already dressed, his still-damp hat in hand. "I went out to the stables to get a horse saddled for you, too."

He pointed to the huge windows at the front of the house, where she could see his bay mare next to a smaller roan. It had stopped raining outside, but the skies remained gray, the heavy clouds still low in the sky.

"Thank you." She slid her hair band off her wrist to tie her hair back. "Although I have to admit, I didn't mind riding double on our way here."

It had been downright sexy, actually.

She saw a flare of heat in his eyes at the shared memory, but then it was gone again, his expression shifting to an easy smile as he opened the front door for her.

"That makes two of us." He palmed her back, guiding her ahead of him outside so they could mount.

Something was definitely wrong.

Determined to confront him about it, to get it out in the open, she turned toward him.

Only to find Carson several steps behind her, his gaze glued to his phone. He stood frozen in place.

"Carson?" Her thoughts shifted away from her worries, knowing he had a lot on his mind right now. "Is it your stepmom? Is everything okay?"

He looked up at her slowly, his blue gaze not quite focused.

"Paige got a letter from the blackmailer today, demanding five million to be deposited to an off-shore account." He gripped his phone tight, his knuckles white.

Her stomach knotted. She couldn't even imagine what he must be feeling.

"Carson, I'm so sorry." She moved to his side to offer whatever comfort she could, but he was rigid as stone when she touched him.

"I need to be with my family." He shoved his hat on his head and pocketed his phone. "I need to get home."

"I'll go with you." She wanted to be there for him the way he'd helped her this week. She had her own bodyguard and a top-of-the-line security system protecting her from her ex-boyfriend, thanks to Carson.

She wasn't even certain that he'd heard her as he headed for his horse and put a foot in his stirrup, but she understood he must be reeling from the news.

She followed suit, moving toward the roan.

Behind her, Carson cursed.

"I'm sorry. I'm not thinking." He appeared at her side, giving her a boost onto the back of the mount, even though he must know she didn't really require a hand. His deeply engrained manners were automatic, even when he was this upset. "If you ride to my father's house with me, I'll let Dax know where you are so he can see you safely back to the Creek Spill."

"But I'm happy to stay with you. I don't have to work today—"

"Thank you, but that won't be necessary." His blue eyes were steely as he stared up at her. "Dax will make sure you get home."

Could he have made it any more plain he didn't want her comfort? Or even her company? Hurt and knowing this wasn't the time to talk about it, she simply nodded.

She would follow Carson to his father's house and wait for the security guard like he'd asked. But it was obvious the risk she'd taken in letting her guard down with him had been a major miscalculation.

Not only had she been unwise in opening herself up to potential hurt, she had also undermined all the hard work she'd done in the last few years to feel emotionally strong. Independent. Because as she nudged her horse into motion to follow Carson across the Wyoming hills, Emma knew she'd lost a piece of her heart to him today. Based on the way he'd retreated from her, he somehow knew that she was falling for him.

And despite the sizzling passion, the feeling simply wasn't returned.

Twenty minutes later, Emma regretted slowing down Carson on the ride to his parents' home. No doubt he could have raced over the rugged but familiar-to-him Wyoming terrain in half the time if he'd been alone, but he maintained a more reasonable pace for her sake. Especially when they'd had to cross streams overflowing from the recent rain, or when they'd had to pick their way down a rocky bluff because it was faster than going around.

He may have withdrawn from her emotionally, but she couldn't fault him for lack of chivalry, even when it was obvious he was worried for his family. As the simple two-story home on the property of the Black Creek Ranch came into view, she did a double take, seeing a man who looked just like Carson stepping out of a big gray pickup truck.

His twin.

When Carson's brother came toward them, Emma could see subtle differences in the way they carried themselves.

She reined in when Carson did, swinging down to the ground before he could help her.

"Carson." His twin nodded at him, his tone brusque.

There was a stiffness about their greeting that Emma suspected might be there even if this wasn't a devastating day for the family.

"Cody." Carson nodded back, his gesture mirroring his brother's. Even their hats were the same. Carson drew her forward. "Emma, this is my brother Cody. Cody, this is Emma Layton. She's a stunt performer."

"A stunt performer?" Cody held out his hand, his blue eyes kind under the brim of his Stetson. "Nice to meet you, Emma. Looks like my daredevil twin has met his match."

"It's nice to meet you, too," she murmured, unsure about his comment since she'd never seen that side of Carson. Had it been a subtle dig? She couldn't help but feel defensive of him, no matter that Carson didn't seem to want her around for the family meeting. "And Carson has been helping me to stay safe during the riding stunts. He's been a good influence."

Cody's eyebrows lifted, his gaze darting to his brother. "Is that right?"

But Carson's attention was on the driveway where another vehicle had pulled up. "Here's Maisie." He turned back to his twin. "You know Scarlett is still in LA, Madeline's at the White Horse and can't get away, and Brock is in Bakersfield for the day. So it's just the three of us for this."

"Emma makes four," Cody pointed out.

Carson tensed beside her. Did the idea of having

her there with his family upset him that much? Or did his reaction have more to do with whatever undercurrent ran between him and his twin?

"You really think Dad will talk in front of anyone who isn't family?" Carson responded tightly.

"He'd probably be glad to have someone sit with Paige," Cody explained. "I would have brought Jillian, but she's battling some fierce morning sickness."

Emma could see some of the tension seep out of Carson's shoulders. How strange to think she could already read his body language that way.

"I'm sorry she's not feeling well." Carson sounded sincere.

"Thank you. She usually perks up later in the day, but I didn't want her to tire herself out more. See you both inside." Cody touched the brim of his Stetson and gave Emma a nod before striding away and into the modest two-story house.

She understood this family meeting wasn't going to be pleasant and she hadn't meant to make things more awkward. "I can still wait out here for Dax, if you prefer."

"It's not that I'm trying to cut you out," Carson assured her, though his eyes didn't quite meet hers as he glanced over to where his sister was walking toward them. "I just wasn't certain how much my father would say in front of you. He only found out about the blackmail note himself just now."

"Well I'm very happy to sit with your stepmother while the rest of your talk if you would like me to," Emma told him, her eyes shifting toward Carson's sister, dressed in worn red cowboy boots, jeans and a dusty T-shirt with the ranch logo printed on it.

Like the other McNeills, her dark hair and bright blue eyes gave her a distinctive look that marked her as family. But there was a no-nonsense clip to her walk and her gaze was frank.

"Yes. My God, yes. Please sit with my mother." Maisie already had a hand out to shake Emma's. "I'm Maisie and thank you for volunteering for that."

Emma liked her already, appreciating the warm welcome after the awkwardness between Carson and his brother.

"Emma Layton." She squeezed Maisie's hand.

"The stunt rider. I attended some of the race scene filming yesterday, and I thought you were fantastic." Maisie flipped her bangs out of her eyes. "Plus, it was sort of refreshing watching my reckless big brother be scared for someone else's neck for a change. In the past it was always us holding our breath to see if he lived through another day." Maisie winked at Carson and looped her arm through Emma's. "Come in and I'll introduce you to Mom. If you can distract her, that would be great. She's been wound up and confused ever since she woke from her coma and I'm sure the latest news isn't helping."

Emma wasn't sure how to refuse, let alone how to

get a word in edgewise with Maisie's nonstop talking. She had a hunch that the other woman was trying to ensure Carson didn't gainsay her, though, so the torrent of words was more to prevent him from interrupting than to silence Emma.

Still, she glanced back at Carson to see if he was frustrated at the way his siblings had coerced him into inviting her inside. But he followed them up the flagstone path, hands shoved in his pocket, his expression inscrutable.

Maybe he didn't want her to come in, but clearly his siblings welcomed the help on a difficult day for the family. And there was something comforting about that, when Carson was pulling away from her as fast as he could.

Because even though her relationship with Carson wasn't going to survive, Emma would never forget the way he'd helped her this week when she'd been at a personal crossroads. His patient teaching had given her the skills needed to keep her job. He'd given her a safe place to be when Austin was released from the state penitentiary.

Best of all, his tenderness and passion had given her a glimpse of what real love should look like. Their time together had proven to her that she'd healed from her past.

So even though what she had with Carson couldn't last, Emma wouldn't trade her time in Cheyenne for anything. And if she could do this small thing to help him in return for all he'd given her, then she would gladly sit with his stepmother all day long.

For all Emma knew, it might be her last chance to be close to Carson McNeill.

Carson put on a fresh pot of coffee in his father's kitchen, listening to his family argue about whether or not to call the police. The kitchen opened onto the living area, so he could still chime in if he chose. But as he filled the glass carafe with filtered water, he wasn't sure where he fell in the debate.

Then again, maybe he was just too damned distracted thinking about Emma. Remembering that hurt look in her eyes when he'd suggested she go home with Dax.

It was a hurt that he'd seen in her eyes even before then, starting when he'd pulled back after making love in the sauna. She'd seen the walls go up. Recognized the withdrawal for what it was, even if she hadn't called him on it. He hadn't ever wanted to cause her pain. But somehow, he was going to do just that.

And now, she was in Paige's bedroom, trying to distract her from the threat of extortion with talk about horses. The weather. The beauty of Wyoming. Carson had wandered past the open door enough times since Emma had gone in there that he knew she was doing a good job of keeping things light.

Keeping Paige from joining the argument in the living room.

That Emma would put his family first touched him, even as it made him more certain he was all wrong for her. She deserved the kind of man who would put her first, too. Someone who wouldn't put her love at risk.

"Carson," his sister called from the living room, "do you think we should call the police?"

"The letter doesn't explicitly say not to," he observed, thinking out loud more than necessarily giving an answer. He went into the living room and picked up the note, which his father had already slid into a plastic bag to preserve as evidence. "It says, 'Paige's secrets will be revealed in the most public possible way, across all social media channels, three days from now at 6 p.m. Pacific time unless five million dollars is sent to an off-shore account. Routing information will arrive at 3 p.m. that day.'"

"And there was no postmark," his father added, his weathered face as worried as Carson had ever seen.

Well, as worried as he'd seen since those horrific days after his birth mother's injury. For the three days that Kara Calderon McNeill had clung to life after being run down by a bull, Donovan had been a shell of a man, his face a mask of fear.

Then, after her death, Donovan McNeill had become someone different. An intense man, fiercely devoted to the ranch and his family, willing to cut off anyone and everyone who threatened either. But he didn't show emotion. Not even when he'd walked away from his own father for good.

For Carson, seeing his father shaken again brought back unwelcome memories. And hammered home the gravity of the family's situation.

"So the letter was left by someone locally." Cody sat in the recliner, but kept his feet planted on the floor, an elbow on each knee. "I still say it's someone on the set of *Winning the West*. Someone who didn't want to film up here in the first place. That's the only explanation that makes sense for why Scarlett got a note in LA, and now we got a note in Cheyenne."

Maisie sat sideways on the love seat, boots off, feet propped on the cushion next to her. "Right. Plus the first note warned us that we shouldn't let the movie film up here. Maybe the blackmailer didn't want Paige to recognize him."

"We only have three days to figure out what we're going to do," Carson reminded them as he headed back into the kitchen. "And we've had a private investigator working on it for five days already."

"Only to come up with nothing," Cody muttered, scratching a hand through his hair.

"He got sidetracked looking into Logan King's background. So far, the actor seems clean, but since Scarlett is in LA again with him, I thought it wise to have someone make sure she stays safe."

Maisie gave a dismissive snort. "Scarlett will lose it if she finds out you're having her followed, do you know that? Lose. It."

Carson hadn't considered that. But damn it, her safety came first.

Their father folded his arms across his barrel chest. "Scarlett aside, do we really think the cops are going to do any better than a PI with the best possible references?"

The coffee maker chimed on the counter, the machine spewing steam as it burbled. Maisie shifted her feet off the love seat to stand, joining Carson in the kitchen.

"Before we go any further, we need to call Granddad," she announced. "This blackmailer isn't just going after Paige. He's going after the McNeills. That involves a lot more people than the ones who live in Cheyenne."

Dad swore. He hadn't spoken to his father in over twenty years. But Carson had hoped that maybe he was ready to put it behind him when Donovan had willingly stepped onto his father's private jet for the flight up to Yellowstone where Paige had been in her hiking accident. Before that, Malcolm McNeill had rented a small hobby ranch in Cheyenne around Christmastime to try to make amends with his son, and he'd kept the house since then in an effort to show he was serious about salvaging their relationship. Carson liked the guy. They all did, actually.

Cody was the lone holdout besides Donovan who hadn't paid a visit to Malcolm's place.

But Cody surprised Carson by backing up Maisie. "She's right. This is bigger than us, Dad. If Mom's past has any kind of scandal that could hurt Malcolm's business, or his other grandkids' businesses, we at least owe him a heads-up."

Maisie poured two cups of coffee and brought one of them—black—to their father. "Here, Dad." She set it down on the coffee table in front of his spot on the sofa. "You really don't have any ideas what Mom might be hiding?"

Donovan shrugged. "She came to Cheyenne to start over. I knew that. Figured she had a dad who beat her or something, with the way she's always been skittish."

Carson ground his teeth. How could his father not know after being married to Paige for so long? Carson had only known Emma a short time, and already he wanted to put walls between her and anyone who wanted to hurt her.

Not just this week, he realized. But for as long as she'd let him. The thought stopped him cold.

"What about her family?" Carson pressed, taking Maisie's forgotten coffee over to her and setting it on the coffee table next to her. "The PI says that no one who shares Paige's maiden name of Samara has ever heard of her in that tiny Canadian town where she said her aunt Mary lives. You don't know anyone else from her past?"

Donovan started to shake his head when a voice from the hallway joined the conversation.

"I do." Emma stood at the edge of the room. She held a round locket in her hand, a necklace Carson recognized as Paige's. "I know the woman pictured in here. And her name isn't Mary."

Twelve

Emma couldn't stop shaking.

She watched as the necklace quivered in her grip, wondering what on earth the locket meant. Whatever it was, she couldn't shake the sense that something bad would come of it.

Carson moved to her side, ushering her into his father's living room. "Is Paige okay?" he asked quietly, his strong arms so incredibly welcome. So grounding. If only she could trust in what she felt. "Should one of us go sit with her?"

"She fell asleep a minute ago," Emma told him, realizing Carson's whole family was staring at her, sitting forward on their seats.

Had she been too quick to run out here to share her discovery with them? She'd just been so…stunned.

Her gaze flicked to the man who must be their father, a big cowboy wearing a leather vest and boots, his blue plaid shirt and jeans giving him the stamp of another era. His arms were folded across his chest as he eyed her skeptically.

Carson's twin sat near him while one of their sisters perched on a heavy coffee table, two cups of java close to her as she swiveled around to have a look at Emma.

"She showed you her locket?" Maisie asked while Carson guided Emma to the sofa.

He sank into the cushion next to her, his presence comforting. Strong. Warm. His touch settled her nerves, making her question her haste to share. She'd never liked feeling anxious—a sensation she associated with her mother, who'd spent whole years of her life being worried. With an effort, Emma took a deep breath.

"Not exactly," Emma admitted, dropping the necklace into Carson's open palm. "Paige was holding on to it when I went into her room. I asked her about it, thinking that was a good topic since Maisie said to distract her."

Maisie nodded, so Emma continued, hoping she hadn't spoken out of turn to divulge a family secret, or to reveal something Paige had kept private. But the McNeills had been through so much. They deserved to know what Emma had learned.

"Paige clutched it tighter, like the locket was meaningful. Then she told me a story about her aunt Mary, who had always struggled with addiction but was actually a sweet person. So I talked a little about my mom—" She slanted a glance toward Carson, trying to remember how much she'd disclosed about her mother. "She's good-hearted, though a bit unstable, even if addiction was never one of her demons."

Carson squeezed her shoulder, and she was tempted to tip her head to rest it briefly on him, as if she could absorb his strength. The conversation with Paige—while brief—had been more draining than she would have anticipated, given that her mission had been to avoid conversational land mines and keep her calm.

But Carson had only gotten involved with her to keep her safe. Not to care for her. Definitely not to love her.

"I don't remember Paige ever saying Aunt Mary was an addict," Carson's twin said. "Dad, did you know that?"

Their father shook his head before he asked, "What else did she say?"

"Not much." Emma tried to remember. "Besides, I was more focused on thinking of topics that weren't related to her past in case that upset her. That's why I brought up my own mother—to maybe redirect her."

"You did well," Carson assured her softly, his palm flat against her back. Rubbing lightly. "Thank you."

She knew she shouldn't take so much comfort from his touch when he had pulled away from her after the sauna. This tenderness he showed her wouldn't last. When her part of the filming was over, Carson wouldn't be clamoring to see her again.

Reluctantly, she straightened, distancing herself ever so slightly.

"Anyway, she fell asleep after that and she dropped the necklace. I picked it up so it didn't get lost in the linens, thinking I'd set it on her dresser, but since the locket was open anyhow, I glanced at the photo inside."

She'd been stunned to recognize the face.

"Who is it?" Carson asked.

"Her name is Barbara Harris. I've seen her photo plenty of times at the Ventura house when I helped my mother clean." Remembering that Carson's family didn't know anything about her, she explained, "My mom is a maid for Emilio Ventura, Antonio's father."

Maisie turned to her dad. "Antonio is the director of *Winning the West*," she explained. "All the Hollywood tabloids say he's a first-rate tool, but his movies make lots of money. And his father, Emilio, was a director before him. They're sort of Hollywood royalty, but neither of them sounds like a particularly nice guy."

"So who the hell is Barbara Harris to the Ventura family?" Donovan McNeill asked, his voice raised with exasperation. "And why is my wife calling this woman Aunt Mary for the last twenty-some years?"

Emma couldn't answer the latter, but she felt compelled to address the former. "I just know that Barbara acted in a lot of B movies that Emilio Ventura directed. Horror flicks and low-budget stuff. Emilio has a framed poster of a zombie film in his office and Barbara's on it."

"Maybe Barbara is a stage name and her real name is Mary," Carson suggested. "Actors don't always use their real names."

Across the room, Cody nodded. "Or Mary could be Barbara's twin," he said drily.

Emma couldn't deny the possibility, given how much Carson and Cody looked alike. But that didn't feel right. Carson had said that Scarlett wanted to ask Emma about the Venturas. There was a connection between the McNeills and the Venturas, she was certain of it.

Maisie took a sip of her coffee. "Or for all we know, Barbara could have worked as a model before she became an actress, and her face was the photo that came inside the damn locket when Mom bought it."

Her sarcasm suggested they were getting off track with all the conjecturing.

Donovan swore softly before he pounded the heel of his hand against his forehead. Once. Twice. "None of this gets us any closer to the truth. And time is ticking. Do we call the cops for help, or not?"

"First, we ask Granddad," Maisie insisted, getting to her feet.

She strode toward the front door with purpose.

"What are you doing?" Donovan asked. Through the picture window behind him Emma could now see an elegantly dressed older couple slowly make their way up the walk.

The woman had long gray hair piled into a chignon and kept in place with a jeweled comb. She held a closed umbrella in one hand and used it like a cane. Next to her, a silver-haired man in a trench coat clutched her arm tightly, though it was unclear which of them supported the other.

Something about the way they touched said they were very much in love, the tenderness so evident it made Emma's heart ache for all that she wouldn't experience with Carson. She couldn't pretend she didn't long for that kind of love.

"I texted your father to come join us," Maisie explained to Donovan McNeill before opening the door. "So your feud with him ends right now, Dad."

Carson had to hand it to his half sister. She didn't pull punches.

He'd been trying for months to convince his father to make peace with Malcolm, to no avail. But Maisie went straight for the jugular. She pulled open the front door of their father's house to admit Malcolm and his girlfriend, Rose Hanson, wrapping each of them in a quick hug.

Cody had been the last holdout among Donovan's kids to smooth things over with their grandfather. Yet even he'd caved last week after Malcolm had offered his plane and pilot at a moment's notice when the family needed to fly to Yellowstone.

Carson reached for Emma's hand and squeezed it, telling himself he needed to protect her in case fireworks broke out between his dad and grandfather. More likely, Carson simply craved her touch on a day that had left him reeling.

It had to be tough for her, too. Talking about her mother's issues in front of his family, people she'd only just met, couldn't have been easy. But she'd done it to try to help solve a mystery that he was chasing around and around his head. His father knew that just the name Ventura upset Paige. Yet he'd remained silent about that in front of the family, not relating last night's episode when Paige hadn't wanted to go to sleep until Antonio Ventura was off McNeill land.

Did his father know more than he was admitting about Paige's past?

But right now, the bigger issue was the McNeill showdown in his father's living room. Cody and Carson rose to greet the older couple at the same time.

Carson introduced Emma to them both. And then, there was nothing to do but see how Donovan reacted.

Carson held his breath during a moment of awkward silence.

Then, slowly, his father rose from his seat.

Donovan's expression revealed nothing as he approached his father.

Rose pressed tighter to Malcolm's side. It was just a hint of movement, but the gesture was so damned endearing. As if this tiny wisp of an eighty-year-old woman was prepared to protect Malcolm from any rejection by his middle-aged son.

Donovan cleared his throat.

"Thank you for coming, Dad," he said finally, belatedly holding out a hand as if to shake.

Malcolm took an awkward step forward, his arms outstretched. "Always."

The two men hugged, clapping each other on the back. Malcolm's eyes squeezed shut, but Rose didn't bother to hide a few tears, her smile wide as she nodded her approval.

"Now." Malcolm straightened, using the back of the recliner to aid his balance. "Let's put our heads together and figure out how to protect that wife of yours, shall we? No worthless blackmailer is going to rip apart the McNeills as long as I draw breath."

An hour later, after much catching up, more coffee and then a rehashing of details about the blackmailing incidents so far, Carson realized his father was leaning toward brazening the whole thing out, come what may for the family.

Donovan didn't want to negotiate, and he didn't want to bend. He wanted to just see what the blackmailer did next.

Malcolm seemed prepared for the worst, although he was making notes about whom to phone so that all of his grandsons could be prepared. Maisie was already searching for publicity firms that could help control the McNeill side of the story if it came to that. Carson thought he should probably take Emma home. He was about to offer when his phone vibrated.

He checked it since the whole room turned to stare at him. They were all on edge after the blackmail letter arrived.

"It's Scarlett," he informed them, his stomach knotting with a new worry. "I'd better take it."

Make sure she was safe.

"I messaged her about the letter," Maisie called over the screen of her laptop as Carson excused himself from the living room to answer the call.

No doubt his youngest half sister was worried about her mother. She probably wanted to come home as soon as possible.

"Scarlett." He moved deeper into the kitchen, so he could still see his family over the breakfast bar, but wouldn't distract them from their conversation. "Everything okay?"

His gaze met Emma's, her attention suddenly turning his way. She must have heard the concern in his voice even though they were in different rooms. That silent connection between them made him think about Rose Hanson pressing close to Carson's grandfather. A wordless gesture of support.

But Carson hadn't earned that kind of support from Emma. He'd sought to protect her from her stalker ex and now it appeared he'd embroiled her in a crisis of his own. Before Emma, he'd always kept relationships simple, with minimal emotional drama. But now, the whole damn world was upside down.

The thought evaporated as Scarlett drew a breath and let loose on him, her voice vibrating through the phone.

"No, in fact it's not at all *okay*," Scarlett practically shouted at him.

"Honey, what's wrong?" He tensed, prepared to fly to California personally to take apart this actor boyfriend if he'd hurt her. Again.

"What's *wrong*?" his half sister asked, as if he ought to know. She sounded frustrated. Angry, actually, more than hurt. "I'll tell you what's wrong, Carson. You hired a private eye to spy on me. Is that your idea of fun? Keeping tabs on me without telling me?"

Ah, damn.

He felt the pinch of guilt, but only for a second. He'd only been looking out for her, a protective instinct drummed into him at a young age.

"Scarlett, I was worried about Logan. I wasn't trying to spy on you. I just wanted to make sure that the guy wasn't the blackmailer."

Was it so damn wrong he needed to keep her safe?

"And you don't trust my judgement on this? Did you listen to a word I said when I saw you last night at the airfield?" Scarlett was always the sweet sister with her butterfly hairclips and bangs, her glittery shoes and whimsical outlook. But right now, she sounded furious. "Did you hop on Gramp's jet two seconds after we spoke and start texting California investigators?"

Emma started to walk his way, perhaps drawn by the tone of his voice. Before she reached the kitchen, however, she stepped out the front door, lifting her own cell to her ear.

Carson turned his attention back to his sister, feeling torn, wanting to know more about the tense expression on Emma's face. "Scarlett, it wasn't like that. I've been working with an investigator to look into the blackmail. I just asked for extra protection for you while you were in LA, since you were obviously targeted by the blackmailer the last time you were there."

And speaking of extra protection, was Dax outside to look after Emma? They weren't on the Creek

Spill property here since his father's home sat on the Black Creek Ranch. Carson had messaged Dax long ago, but the guard might have left since then.

He hated to interrupt Scarlett. But she seemed okay. She only wanted to vent about Logan getting into a scrap with the guy when he'd caught him lurking around his place in Malibu. Then she threatened to move to the West Coast and not speak to Carson again.

"Honey, I'm sorry," he tried to interject gently while he moved toward the front door. "Truly, I am. But things are falling apart here, and I need to check on Emma. I can call you back—"

He realized before he finished the sentence that his volatile half sister had hung up on him. Cursing under his breath, he pocketed the phone and stepped outside. It had started to rain again, the clouds from earlier having lingered all day.

And there was no sign of Emma.

Fear chilled his gut. Just a little at first.

Remembering what her ex had done to her made his fists clench. Clearing his throat, he shouted her name. "Emma?"

He jogged out the driveway to get a better view of the yard and still didn't see her, so he called again, "Emma, where are you? Emma!"

Only silence answered his call, turning his fear into a solid ball of ice.

Thirteen

Inside Donovan McNeill's small stable, Emma strained to hear the caller on the other end of the bad connection. The storm must have something to do with it. She'd only come in here to take the call because a few fat raindrops hit her on her way out the door. Now, the rain was falling in earnest.

"Hello?" she said again, double-checking caller ID even though she knew she didn't recognize the number.

When she'd picked up, she figured it was a client, or potential client, contacting her about the personal training services she offered. Of course, there was always the hope that it could be a casting agent booking her for another stunt job. Plenty of people did business from their cell phones and didn't list the numbers.

"How long do you think you can hide from me, Emma?"

The threatening male voice on the other end was unmistakably familiar.

Austin.

Emma told herself to hang up. But fear seemed to have invaded her limbs, making them immobile. Robbing her of speech.

Memories of her ex-boyfriend rushed through her, the shock of him punching her. The momentary confusion that came when someone you thought cared about you suddenly turned into an ugly stranger, capable of anything. An old hint of that confusion returned now, making a mockery of everything she'd done to protect herself. To feel strong.

"I know where you are, Emma," the voice crooned in a way that made her stomach heave. "And I'm coming for you."

The fear chilled her as her knees seemed to give out. With a shaking hand, she stabbed the end button on her phone, disconnecting the call. She staggered against the rough stable wall, a board snagging her tank top and scratching her shoulder.

The pain—however small—helped chase away that frozen feeling, the hurt reminding her that she had battled through so much pain and fear these last three years. She was strong. She stepped into knife fights for fun, for crying out loud. That was her job now.

Being fearless. Being tough.

She wouldn't let him hurt her again.

"Emma!"

She became aware of another voice outside the stable, calling to her through the storm. A far more welcome voice.

Carson.

Relief made her dizzy. She dragged in a breath of air scented with clean hay and horses, then cracked open the stable door to call out to Carson. The rain had slowed to a light patter.

"In here!" she shouted, willing her heart rate to return to normal as she ducked back into the stable.

She had to pull herself together to face Carson. She didn't want him to see how the call had rattled her. And while it would be easy to lose herself in his strong arms, and to forget all about being independent for a little while, she couldn't afford to do that. She had calls to make—the police, the parole board, her roommate, a lawyer? She didn't know. She needed a private space to assess her options and figure out her next move.

Swallowing down the wild flux of emotions, Emma busied herself with saddling the roan mare Carson had given her to ride from Brock's house. She needed something to do with her nervous hands and the roan was already whinnying impatiently in her stall. Emma led her out of the stall and toward the tacking area, glad for the activity when she was cracking under the pressure of too many feelings.

"Emma." Carson burst in through the stable door, his shirt wet with scattered raindrops, making the cotton cling. "Are you okay? What are you doing?"

"I'm fine," she assured him, though her voice gave her away with a tremble. "But I need to get back to the house. I—um. I have some business to take care of."

She reached for the saddle, but Carson rushed over to take it from her, settling it on the horse for her.

"Will you wait a second? What business?" He studied her face, his eyes full of concern.

But damn it, the concern wasn't because he loved her. It was that protective streak, too engrained to ignore. And this wasn't his battle. It was hers. She busied herself with the bridle, positioning the straps as she murmured soothingly to the horse.

Or to herself.

"Emma?" Carson prodded when she didn't answer right away, his hands automatically tightening the girth, helping her with the bit. "What business? I can tell you're upset."

"I am upset," she told him, as calmly as she could when she was scared and hurting inside. But she wasn't her mother and she wouldn't fly into a panic. "My ex-boyfriend just phoned me, and I need to file a police report."

Carson's hands fell away from the roan. He turned to Emma, his shoulders tense. "My God, Emma. How did he get your number? Does he know where you are?"

He reached for her, but Emma couldn't let herself fall into his arms, even though everything inside her shouted at her to take the comfort he offered. She stood tall, her hand on the reins.

She really needed to leave before she dissolved into a mass of emotions in front of him. She'd already been battling heartbreak and rejection this morning after the way Carson had pulled back from her at his brother's house. It had been all she could do to hold it together in front of the McNeills. But now? Her reserves were gone after that call from Austin. She needed to get away from here, fast. Before she revealed how hard she'd fallen for a man who was more interested in being her protector than her lover.

"I don't know how he got the number," she admitted. "He said he knows where I am, but he didn't taunt me with the information, which makes me think he's bluffing. If he knew where I was, he wouldn't waste time calling me to warn me."

She backed up a step, toeing open the stable doors so she could mount up and make a tactical retreat. She just couldn't face having Carson insist on staying around her out of some protective sense of obligation.

"Emma." Carson stepped in front of her, his

big body blocking her path. “You’re not thinking straight. What if he’s out there, waiting for you?”

She bristled at the move. “He’s not. And if he is, that’s my business. From now on, I protect myself. Your protective services are no longer required. I will update the police and let them take care of the matter.”

The rain had stopped, and a cool breeze was blowing from the north. She needed that fresh air to clear her head. Needed the cold wind to ease the burn in her chest.

“I don’t understand.” Carson touched her shoulder, his hand a gentle warmth she still craved. “Whatever you’re angry with me for, please don’t use it as an excuse to put yourself in a dangerous situation.”

“Carson, if I wasn’t in a dangerous position, would you even be out here talking to me?” How had she gone from a relationship with a man who hit her to a relationship with a man who was only with her to protect her? “Thank you for helping me with my riding, but I’m not longer your responsibility.”

“Yes, you are.” His blue eyes narrowed. “You’re still on my land. You’re still at risk, only this time it’s a lunatic ex-boyfriend and not a horse that’s threatening you.”

“So shut down the filming. Send me packing.” She couldn’t do this with him anymore. Wouldn’t put her heart in his hands only to have him go back to being a polite stranger once she was safe again. “That would be kinder to me than making me care about you, only to pull away afterward like we had just a meaningless one-night stand. I'm not that woman, Carson. I won't be."

Putting a toe in the stirrup, she swung her leg over the roan's back and urged the twitchy mare forward.

Fast.

She squeezed the quarter horse's sides gently with her legs, propelling her more.

Carson's shout faded in the distance behind her.

Rain-washed air whooshed past Emma's face as she leaned over the roan's head, the horse's mane fluttering against her cheek. The wind dried her tears.

She'd been wrong about the cool breeze soothing the burn in her chest, though. Nothing was going to take away the suffering in her heart that had Carson's name all over it. She'd been such a fool to move in to his house. Welcome him into her bed.

But oh, hell, she couldn't regret those beautiful moments with him—in Jackson last night and again today in the sauna. She wouldn't trade that for anything.

No matter that it hurt now and always would.

She pulled the reins lightly to the right, seeing a muddy patch ahead. But the mare leaped it easily. Just when her hooves hit the ground again, however, lighting flashed in the sky.

Thunder rumbled at almost the same moment.

All at once, the horse spooked.

The mare dropped her shoulder, spinning to one side.

The movement was too fast for Emma. She couldn't do any of the maneuvers Carson had taught her. She lost her seat too quickly, flying through the air.

Coming down on her back with a sickening thud.

Carson didn't bother saddling the bay to go after Emma. He sprinted into the equipment shed and fired up his father's ATV. He didn't know where Dax was and didn't take the time to text the security guard. If Emma's maniac ex-boyfriend was out there, Carson didn't have a second to waste.

Roaring out into the woods, he hadn't gone far when the roan Emma had been riding came trotting out of the trees.

Riderless.

Carson's mind filled with a dozen scenarios and none of them were good. His gut sank.

Fear howled through him. His chest felt like it would implode as he squeezed the last bit of speed out of the ATV, pushing the thing as fast as it could go. He flew over bumps, kicking up leaves and branches as he tore through mud, following the trail the horse had left in the muddy path.

Until he spotted Emma lying on the ground, her body contorted at a strange angle.

Horror flooded him, past and present mingling as a memory of his mother's body lying prone in the cattle pen flashed in front of his eyes.

It had been his worst nightmare then, and one he couldn't accept repeating. He must have shut off the ATV, because the next thing he knew, he was running to her side. That was when he became aware of another man on the periphery of the clearing.

"Don't move her," the man shouted. "I'm calling 911."

The ex-boyfriend?

A momentary red haze passed over Carson's vision as he turned toward the guy. But it was Dax, the security guard. He must have followed her out here, doing the job he'd been assigned. Carson blinked through the confusion, his focus returning to Emma.

"Carson?"

Her voice was whisper soft, but the word was distinct.

His heart lodged in his throat while, behind him, Dax shouted out directions to the emergency dispatch.

"I'm here." Carson kneeled on the damp ground beside her. "You're going to be fine," he assured her, needing it to be true even if her legs were twisted awkwardly beneath her. No wonder Dax didn't want her moved until EMS got here.

Carson tried not to remember the way his mother had clung to life for three interminable days when they'd careened between hope and despair. He shook off the past, needing to be here for Emma now.

Gently, he brushed a strand of brown hair out of her eyes, but it caught in her lashes.

"The thunder…" Emma's eyes opened for a moment, unfocused. "It spooked her."

He pressed his forehead to hers, willing her to be all right. He didn't see any blood outside of some surface scratches, but that didn't rule out internal injuries.

"I know, honey. It's okay. And you're going to be okay, too. Help is coming."

"The roan—" she began, her eyebrows furrowed in question.

"She's fine. She was already trotting home when I came to find you." He wanted to wrap Emma up in his arms, even though it was too late to keep her safe.

He just wanted *her*.

Needed her.

He loved this woman too damn much for anything to happen to her. Love? Why the hell hadn't he figured that out sooner, when he could have said it to her back at his father's stable? Before she rode away and…

Eyes stinging, he closed them against the pain as he kissed her forehead.

"Emma?" He wanted to tell her now. To assure her that he cared, and not just because he wanted to protect her.

But as his gaze returned to hers, her eyes were closed. Her mouth had gone slack. Thankfully, he could feel the reassuring puff of her breath on his cheek.

She'd passed out, but she was still right there with him.

Still alive.

Carson ground his teeth, willing her to stay that way.

Fourteen

Waiting was enough to drive a man insane.

Carson paced the corridor at the hospital in Cheyenne three hours later, hoping the latest doctor who was in with Emma would give the all clear for him to see her. He wasn't a relative of hers, so privacy laws meant he couldn't have immediate access to updates. Which killed him. Especially since EMS had strapped her to a board to move her, a technique that made him fear paralysis.

But about ninety minutes after the ambulance brought Emma into the medical center, her condition was listed as stable.

Not critical.

He kept reminding himself of that when he couldn't

be in there with her, holding her hand. Watching over her himself. This wasn't a situation like with his mother. Emma really was going to be okay.

"You want to talk about it?" Cody asked him from a seat by the window in the waiting room, careful to keep his gaze on some point on the horizon outside and not on Carson.

Carson hadn't spoken much to his twin over the last years—they had too many fundamental differences. But Cody had been one of the first on the scene in the woods after Carson had found Emma. Cody had kept him from coming unglued when the EMS team refused to let him in the ambulance.

And yeah, it was Cody who had to know exactly why seeing Emma on the ground today had been the second most terrifying moment of his life. They'd both been there when their mother had been trampled.

"Talking. Isn't that like pouring acid on a wound?" Carson asked, not slowing his pacing as he glared at the door to Emma's room, willing the doctor to come out with a positive report.

The rest of the family had remained behind at Black Creek Ranch after the ambulance drove off with Emma, since the crisis was still unfolding with the blackmailer. Dax had driven to the hospital in his own vehicle, and remained on duty now, outside the emergency room.

Just in case.

But Carson had already called the cops to let them know about Emma's ex. She could make a more detailed complaint when she awoke. For now, Carson wanted the wheels in motion to find the guy and throw his ass back in prison for contacting her—a clear parole violation and a threatening move that had no doubt rocked her concentration in the saddle.

"Right. Maybe it is," Cody acknowledged, rising from his chair to stand in Carson's path. They stood nose-to-nose for a second before Cody grabbed Carson's shoulders. "Would you consider listening then?"

For a second, memories of similar standoffs blended together with the present one. Times Cody had held him back when Carson wanted to brawl with some kid in high school. Times Cody had tried to talk him out of hopping on the back of a bull too soon after an injury.

So many times his twin had been the responsible one, the cautious one.

Funny how knowing Emma gave Carson a window into his brother's frustration. It hurt to see people you care about put their neck on the line.

"Yes," Carson agreed, dropping to sit in one of the cheap waiting room chairs. "But only until I see Emma's door open."

Cody lowered himself into a seat across from him, his eyes taking Carson's measure.

"Okay. Then I'll come right to the point." Cody laced his fingers together, elbows on the arms of his chair. "I know what happened today had to have sucked the soul right out of you."

He didn't have the emotional resources for this. Not now. "I can't do this—"

His brother continued speaking right over him. "But she's *okay*, and it's obvious she cares about you. Don't screw things up by doing something stupid like pushing her away if you care about her, too."

For the first time in a long time, Carson looked his brother in the eye. Really looked at him.

And let out a surprise bark of laughter.

"What?" Cody frowned, leaning back in his seat.

"I was just thinking that having a conversation with you is exactly like wrestling with my conscience," Carson admitted, hating every minute spent in a hospital waiting room. Too many bad memories. "And then I remembered another time when you were doling out life wisdom when we were just little punks and I screamed at you, 'Who died and left you boss?'"

Cody rolled his eyes, but there was the barest hint of a smile on his lips. "Here we go."

"And without missing a beat, you shouted back, 'Mom did.'" Carson couldn't hold back a grin. "I believed that for a little while, you know."

"Probably because I was always so much smarter

than you," Cody said, glancing up at an orderly jogging past while pushing a wheelchair down the hall.

"Not smarter. Just much less fun." Carson took a small amount of comfort from the lifelong argument, the way they'd set themselves apart from one another when they were actually—truth be told—far too much alike.

"But are you going to listen to me for once?" Cody pressed, not getting sidetracked by the old disagreement. "Admit that I might know best, and that you shouldn't push away someone you care about just because loving someone is a riskier proposition than anything else you've tackled?"

Carson wasn't ready to admit to his brother that he was already committed. If he could explain to Emma how much he cared—if she believed him—he wasn't giving her up. Emma deserved to be the first person to know that.

Besides, Carson had a question for his twin.

"Is that what happened with Jillian?" he asked. "You decided it was worth the risk even though she—"

He hesitated, knowing the mother of Cody's future child was a breast cancer survivor of two years. She'd been the location scout who had chosen McNeill lands as a good potential spot for filming *Winning the West*, a job she'd taken to see the world. She'd asked Cody to travel with her for a few months before their baby was born, and he was actively plan-ning the trip with her. It was a big compromise for someone so focused on his business.

"—is a cancer survivor?" Cody didn't shy away from it. "Hell yes. She's worth the risk. Because the alternative is not being with her, and that's something I refuse to consider."

Carson understood all too well. He didn't want to spend any more time without Emma, either. His half sister's words floated around his brain just then, and he figured Cody would get a kick out of them.

"Maisie said you only dated women you wanted to marry, and I only dated women that I was sure I wouldn't."

Cody laughed. "Sisters have a way with words."

Carson winced. "Speaking of which, I may have screwed up with Scarlett by hiring additional security for her in LA." His gut knotted as he remembered how upset she'd been. "She was angry I hadn't told her. She threatened to pack up and move down there, and it didn't make matters any better that the call came at the same time Emma stepped out of the house and I was distracted."

"I'll get in touch with her," Cody assured him. "You concentrate on Emma."

Carson was about to thank him when the door to Emma's room opened. A short, balding doctor stepped out, holding a chart in one hand.

"Friends of Emma Layton?" the guy asked, peering over the rims of narrow eyeglasses.

Carson was on his feet. “How is she? Can I see her?”

Cody was behind him, a silent shadow. Welcome support.

“She’s doing well, and she asked for you,” the doc replied, glancing back down at the chart. “Assuming you’re Carson?”

The fresh wave of relief nearly leveled him. It was all good news, and still, he felt like he’d been treading water for days and just got pulled into the rescue boat. Cody clapped him on the shoulder.

“I’m Carson.” He tried to focus on the doctor as the guy warned him about concussion symptoms and the need to keep Emma quiet and stress-free. He was glad Cody was there to listen, too, and help him remember everything later.

“No broken bones?” Carson asked, remembering how twisted she’d looked when she fell.

“Nothing is broken. Her arm is scraped up, but her X-rays came back clear.” The doctor went on to suggest her stunt work might have helped her to fall in a way that saved her.

Relief rushed through Carson. “So I can see her?”

“Of course.” The doctor stepped aside. “I’ll get her discharge paperwork started.”

Emma could go home. Carson couldn’t process anything else as he charged toward the door to her room.

He just hoped like hell that going home meant going with him.

* * *

Emma could hear Carson's voice in the hallway.

She was awake now. And conscious.

So surely she couldn't be dreaming his voice. Dreaming of him. He must have come to the hospital to see her. Judging from the tone of his voice, he was anxious to be with her, in fact.

Then again, she had to be dreaming.

Because earlier today, he'd pulled away from her after they'd made love in the sauna. All the intense heat and passion had vanished. He'd given her an easygoing smile, like they were just flirting.

He'd told her she didn't need to come with him to his father's house. That it was unnecessary.

He hadn't wanted to be with her, and she wasn't going to put herself in a situation where her heart would get broken. Not when she'd only just managed to scrape her life back together after the way Austin had messed with her head. Her self-esteem.

"Emma?" Carson's voice was closer now.

Filled with tenderness.

She forced her eyes open, willing herself to face whatever happened next. Because if she'd learned one thing about herself since the day Austin's fist smashed into her face, it was that she wasn't a quitter. And she didn't scare easily.

She'd already called the local police to report Austin, and had received a reassuring message just a few minutes ago that Austin had already been picked up in Los Angeles in an unrelated incident that the sheriff's office wasn't at liberty to disclose. Thank goodness. He'd never been in Cheyenne.

Now Carson sat beside her bed, his chair pulled up as close to the edge as it could be.

"How are you feeling?" he asked, his blue eyes searching her face.

"Better than you might think." She didn't want him to sugarcoat how he treated her in order to keep her safe. "I appreciate you being here, Carson, but the doctor said I'll be fine." When he didn't respond right away, she tried to make her point more clearly. "You don't need to worry about me anymore. Austin is already back in police custody, and I'm returning to the White Canyon Ranch for the rest of the filming."

The words were her declaration of independence. She needed to show him she could stand on her own.

Still, they left her feeling hollow inside. She wanted more than anything to take shelter in his arms for one more day.

Or for a lifetime.

She closed her eyes for a moment, because just thinking about that made her chest constrict with anguish and she refused to let him see her cry. When she opened her eyes again, Carson's face was a mask of—she didn't know what. But his expression was unlike any other one she'd seen.

"If that's really what you want, Emma, I will do whatever I can to make the move easier for you." His words sounded wooden. As hollow as she felt inside. Then, he leaned closer and his hand grazed her arm, his expression shifting into something more real. More…urgent. "But I'd give anything for a chance to do things over today. To rewind to the sauna, and just stay there like we were."

She definitely couldn't think about that. Not with her head still aching from a fall and all her defenses crumbling. "I don't think either of us are the kind of people who would be content with just a physical relationship."

"That's not what I meant. At all." He lowered his voice. "I just know that everything went to hell when we came out of there. I didn't expect to feel so much so fast and I didn't know what to do with that—"

A nurse breezed into the room, staring at her paperwork, dark ponytail bobbing. "I hear someone's ready to go home."

Talk about timing. Emma sighed inwardly.

The woman, dressed in bright blue scrubs and a friendly smile, moved around the bed on the opposite side from Carson. She directed her attention to him. "I'm just going to pull off the monitors and go over the discharge instructions with Emma. Do you want to bring your car around while I call the orderly? We're going to take her down in a wheelchair because of the concussion."

Carson looked back to her, his eyes troubled. "Emma, is that okay with you?"

She had to return to the ranch one way or the other. And she couldn't deny she wanted to hear whatever he'd been about to say before the nurse walked in.

"Yes." At her nod, he straightened from her bedside.

"I'll see you outside then." He lingered for a moment—or was she imagining that?

She didn't imagine the tender kiss he brushed along her forehead, though, gentle as a whisper.

The nurse's eyebrows rose as Carson strode out the door. The woman—Celeste, according to her name tag—gave Emma a conspiratorial wink.

"Handsome fella you've got there," she observed, making some notes on her papers. "You let him take good care of you, honey, after the day you've had."

Emma knew it would be too easy to just forget about her reservations and do just that. But one way or another, she needed to find out if there were deeper feelings behind Carson's protective streak.

Night had fallen.

Emma tipped her throbbing head against Carson's truck seat as he drove out of the hospital parking lot. No matter what else happened tonight—if she ended up returning to her accommodations at the White Canyon Ranch—she'd need to pick up her things from Carson's house first.

They drove in silence for a few moments as Carson steered northwest out of town, toward the Creek Spill.

The rain had cleared, leaving the night sky full of stars. A twinkling canopy perfect for wishing.

But Emma knew this was the real world, and just wishing for Carson's affection wasn't going to make it happen.

"Are you warm enough?" Carson had given her the blanket he kept in the jump seat.

"I feel fine, just a little sore," she assured him. "But I'd like to return to what we were talking about before the nurse came in." Even if it hurt, she needed to know what Carson was feeling. "All afternoon, when we were with your family, I was trying not to think about how you'd pulled away from me. How you hadn't even wanted me to join you at your father's house in the first place, but Maisie kind of invited me anyway."

"It wasn't that I didn't want you there, Emma," he told her firmly, glancing her way as he rolled to a stop at a four-way intersection.

She waved off the semantics impatiently. "You wanted to give us space then, Carson. Please don't deny it because it was glaringly obvious. I know what I saw, and I know how you behaved."

"I pulled away after the sauna because I knew I was in over my head," he told her then, not mincing words. "I felt myself sliding into deeper feelings and that's—not something that I let happen to me."

That hurt so much it left her breathless.

On the one hand, he'd neatly vindicated her argument. She now understood the situation too damned well.

She'd be spending the night at the White Canyon Ranch after all, so she could nurse her broken heart without an audience. Before she could tell him that, he continued to speak, seemingly unaware of the hurt he'd caused.

"My whole life," he said, staring out the windshield at the dark road ahead, "I've avoided meaningful relationships with women. I wasn't even very aware of it until Maisie pointed it out to me this week." He drummed his fingers on the steering wheel, a frustrated pounding. "I'm not proud of being shallow with people. I've just been focused on other things. My career. Healing from all the bull riding mishaps."

She found it difficult to reconcile the image he painted with the man she knew. But she'd had hints of that reputation. She recalled how his family thought of him as the reckless twin while his brother was the responsible one.

"I'm the last person to judge someone based on their prior relationships," she said drily.

Because even if Carson didn't love her, she still found a lot to admire about him. He was a good man. A kind and giving man. He'd spent days helping her improve her riding when he could have just as easily told Zoe that Emma was unfit for the stunt.

"I never gave much thought to what I was doing. I was just—living. Doing my thing." His voice sounded tight. Tense. "But I know now—after seeing what happened today—I was keeping people at arm's length to avoid the kind of hurt that my mom's death caused."

She hadn't expected that. She glanced at him in the dim light of the dashboard as he turned into the long driveway that led to the Creek Spill Ranch. Carson's face was pale. Serious.

Certain.

"I know you lost your father at a young age, too, in a traumatic way." He turned to look at her now that they were on the quiet access road. "So maybe you can relate when it comes back to hurt in new and surprising ways, even years later when you thought you had it handled."

"You never handle it," she admitted. Understanding.

Her throat burned with empathy for Carson and the boy he'd been. And for the pain her accident must have caused him today. She hadn't really put that together until now.

"Never," Carson agreed. "And when I saw your horse trotting back toward my father's stable without you today, I had about fifty simultaneous realizations, all while I was scared out of my mind for you."

As much as she hated to think about what her actions had put him through, she couldn't deny a small flicker of hope at his words. Because being scared out of your mind wasn't the kind of emotion you had for people unless you cared about them.

"I'm sorry I went out on the horse. I should have never done that when I was so upset." She knew better. "I was just so afraid of falling apart in front of you."

"You don't have anything to apologize for. I hurt you today, and I regret that more than I can ever say. But seeing you in the woods, and knowing you'd been thrown, brought back a whole other nightmare." He stopped the truck, making her realize they were in front of the main house at the Creek Spill Ranch.

She blinked back tears, regretting what he'd gone through. Wishing she hadn't gone out on horseback. Slipping off her seat belt, she turned toward him in the darkened cab.

She covered his hand with hers, squeezing.

"And it was…bad." He slid off his seat belt, too, and shifted closer. "But I realized that I'd been trying to avoid that kind of hurt my whole life. Yet when it happened, when I was confronted with the worst scenario, I decided that living in a vacuum and having shallow relationships had all been a giant waste. I hadn't avoided hurt. I'd just wasted a whole lot of time with people who didn't matter much to me."

Emma listened carefully, trying to follow what

he was saying, knowing that her accident had had a strong impact on him. She could hear it in his voice. See the depth of feeling in his blue eyes.

She clutched the binding of the wool blanket tighter, wishing she figured more into his revelation but knowing she couldn't wish his love into happening.

"I understand," she said finally, her voice hoarse with unspoken emotions.

"Not yet, you don't. Because I haven't told you the most important part. I kept thinking, what if I lost you before I got to tell you how much you mean to me? Before I got a chance to tell you that I'm all-in for this." He gestured back and forth between them. "For *you*. For us being together."

That sounded…so good.

Could she trust those words? Especially on a day when she'd hit her head?

"I don't want to misunderstand." She heard the break in her voice. Knew she was showing all the emotions that she'd tried to lock down earlier today in the stable. But he seemed to be sharing his, so she wasn't going to hide hers. She licked her lips and tried again. "I worry the concussion is making me confused."

Carson took both her hands in his.

"Then I'm going to say this very simply." He leaned closer to her, his eyes locked on hers. "You are the most important person in my whole world,

Emma Layton. I'm falling in love with you. Please don't leave me. Not tonight. Not ever."

Hope sparked into full flame, roaring through her with a bright glow. She leaned her forehead against his, the motion dislodging a tear to roll down her cheek.

"I don't want to leave." She edged closer to him, until he slid her carefully onto his lap. "Because, truth be told, I'm falling in love with you, too."

Sitting in his truck, wrapped in his arms, felt like the sweetest homecoming she'd ever had. She tipped her cheek to his shoulder, and he wrapped his arms around her.

"I'm so glad you're okay. And I'm so damn glad you're here with me." He said the words into her hair while he stroked her back.

The fear and tension of the day drained away. Hope and love for this man flowed over her.

"I know it's soon to feel so much—" she began.

"Is it?" Carson edged back to look at her, a smile hitching at his lips. "Maybe it's just that what we have is so much more powerful than what other people have, it's too strong to deny."

She smiled, too, happy from the inside out. Happy because he was.

"Maybe it is," she agreed, looping her arms around his neck.

"My brother told me tonight that you shouldn't push someone away just because love is a risky proposition." Carson stroked her cheek as he gazed into her eyes.

"Wise advice. And since when do we fear risk?"

He laughed. "Never. But let's take future risks together, okay? At least whenever possible?"

"No more being the reckless twin?" she asked.

"No. From now on, I'm only taking calculated risks."

"Such as?"

"Sex without a condom?"

It was her turn to laugh. "You wild man. I'm not sure I can help you with that one. It's going to be difficult enough following doctor's orders to avoid too much excitement while I heal."

Carson's expression turned serious. "No trips to the sauna for a while. I will make sure we follow directions to the letter to get you well. That much, I promise you."

She fell a little more in love with him. It was going to be so easy to fall deeper every day. Even with a concussion. And doctor's orders not to get excited.

"Will you take me home now?" she whispered, brushing kisses along his jaw.

He captured her chin in his hand, his touch tender. "I'm going to love watching over you all night long."

Her heart gave a contented sigh.

He kissed her thoroughly, threading his fingers into her hair, capturing her lips with his. Boldly claiming her, sealing their commitment to make this work. Because a future without him? Well, that wasn't one she wanted to consider.

When he edged back to look at her, she laid her hand on his chest, his heart pounding as fast and hard as hers.

"Remember when you said you wished we could rewind this day?"

"Go back to after the sauna and do it all over? I remember."

"I don't want a do-over since I don't think today turned out so badly after all." She snuggled closer, resting her cheek on his shoulder again, already looking forward to when her head was less fuzzy and she could lose herself in him.

Carson kissed her forehead before reaching behind her to lever open the passenger door. "You're the best thing that ever happened to me, Emma Layton."

She closed her eyes, feeling a wave of tiredness mingling with the happiness.

"Mmm. I second that," she told him as he carried her inside. Across the threshold. Ready for a fresh start. "You're an amazing development in my life, too."

He brought her up the stairs and paused.

"Where would you feel most comfortable?"

She glanced between her door and his. "Would you mind if I sleep in your bed?"

His feet were already heading that way.

"I'm going to do everything in my power to make

you choose that every day for the rest of your life." He backed into the dim room and settled her in the middle of his mattress.

She closed her eyes, and for an instant, an image of Paige McNeill's locket flashed through her mind, bringing a wave of fresh anxiety. She needed to call her mother. To ask what she knew about the troubled actress Barbara Harris. Emma would do anything she could to help Carson find answers about his stepmother's mysterious past.

To help them locate a blackmailer.

But for tonight, she only needed to revel in the love of the best man she knew.

"Do you think kissing would be too much excitement for me?" She wanted to wrap herself around him and fall asleep that way.

Reaching for him, she pulled him down next to her.

"Just for a minute. And then you need your rest," he warned, in his most overprotective voice.

Making her smile.

"That's sixty whole seconds, you know. Don't cheat me of a single one." She pressed herself to him, looking forward to every day with Carson McNeill.

He tilted her face to his, his eyes blazing with an emotion no woman could miss.

"Never," he promised.

* * * * *

Brock McNeill steps up to find the blackmailer before scandal wreaks havoc in the family, but will a beautiful actress with secrets of her own derail him before he can uncover the truth?

Don't miss the final installment of the McNeill Magnates,

One Night Scandal

Available September 2018 from Joanne Rock and Harlequin Desire.

If you're on Twitter, tell us what you think of Harlequin Desire! #harlequindesire

COMING NEXT MONTH FROM

HARLEQUIN® Desire

Available September 4, 2018

#2611 KEEPING SECRETS

Billionaires and Babies • by Fiona Brand

Billionaire Damon Smith's sexy assistant shared his bed and then vanished for a year. Now she's returned—with his infant daughter! Can he work through the dark secrets Zara's still hiding and claim the family he never knew he wanted?

#2612 RUNAWAY TEMPTATION

Texas Cattleman's Club: Bachelor Auction
by Maureen Child

When Caleb attends a colleague's wedding, the last person he expects to leave with is the runaway bride! He offers Shelby a temporary hideout on his ranch. But soon the sizzle between them has this wealthy cowboy wondering if seduction will convince her to stay...

#2613 STRANGER IN HIS BED

The Masters of Texas • by Lauren Canan

Brooding Texan Wade Masters brings his estranged wife home from the hospital with amnesia. This new, sensual, *kind* Victoria makes him feel things he never has before. But when he discovers the explosive truth, will their second chance at love be as doomed as their first?

#2614 ONE NIGHT SCANDAL

The McNeill Magnates • by Joanne Rock

Actress Hannah must expose the man who hurt her sister. Sexy rancher Brock has clues, but amnesia means he can't remember them—or his one night with her! Still, he pursues her with a focus she can't resist. What happens when he finds out everything?

#2615 THE RELUCTANT HEIR

The Jameson Heirs • by HelenKay Dimon

Old-money heir Carter Jameson has a family who thrives on deceit. He's changing that by finding the woman who knows devastating secrets about his father. The problem? He wants her, maybe more than he wants redemption. And what he thinks she knows is nothing compared to the truth...

#2616 PLAYING MR. RIGHT

Switching Places • by Kat Cantrell

CEO Xavier LeBlanc must resist his new employee—his inheritance is on the line! But there's more to her than meets the eye...because she's working undercover to expose fraud at his charity. Too bad Xavier is falling faster than her secrets are coming to light...

YOU CAN FIND MORE INFORMATION ON UPCOMING HARLEQUIN® TITLES, FREE EXCERPTS AND MORE AT WWW.HARLEQUIN.COM.

HDCNM0818

Get 4 FREE REWARDS!

We'll send you 2 FREE Books plus 2 FREE Mystery Gifts.

Harlequin® Desire books feature heroes who have it all: wealth, status, incredible good looks... everything but the right woman.

YES! Please send me 2 FREE Harlequin® Desire novels and my 2 FREE gifts (gifts are worth about $10 retail). After receiving them, if I don't wish to receive any more books, I can return the shipping statement marked "cancel." If I don't cancel, I will receive 6 brand-new novels every month and be billed just $4.55 per book in the U.S. or $5.24 per book in Canada. That's a savings of at least 13% off the cover price! It's quite a bargain! Shipping and handling is just 50¢ per book in the U.S. and 75¢ per book in Canada*. I understand that accepting the 2 free books and gifts places me under no obligation to buy anything. I can always return a shipment and cancel at any time. The free books and gifts are mine to keep no matter what I decide.

225/326 HDN GMYU

Name (please print)

Address   Apt. #

City   State/Province   Zip/Postal Code

Mail to the **Reader Service:**
IN U.S.A.: P.O. Box 1341, Buffalo, NY 14240-8531
IN CANADA: P.O. Box 603, Fort Erie, Ontario L2A 5X3

Want to try two free books from another series? Call 1-800-873-8635 or visit www.ReaderService.com.

*Terms and prices subject to change without notice. Prices do not include applicable taxes. Sales tax applicable in N.Y. Canadian residents will be charged applicable taxes. Offer not valid in Quebec. This offer is limited to one order per household. Books received may not be as shown. Not valid for current subscribers to Harlequin Desire books. All orders subject to approval. Credit or debit balances in a customer's account(s) may be offset by any other outstanding balance owed by or to the customer. Please allow 4 to 6 weeks for delivery. Offer available while quantities last.

Your Privacy—The Reader Service is committed to protecting your privacy. Our Privacy Policy is available online at www.ReaderService.com or upon request from the Reader Service. We make a portion of our mailing list available to reputable third parties that offer products we believe may interest you. If you prefer that we not exchange your name with third parties, or if you wish to clarify or modify your communication preferences, please visit us at www.ReaderService.com/consumerschoice or write to us at Reader Service Preference Service, P.O. Box 9062, Buffalo, NY 14240-9062. Include your complete name and address.

HD18

SPECIAL EXCERPT FROM
HARLEQUIN® Desire

When Caleb attends a colleague's wedding, the last person he expects to leave with is the runaway bride! He offers Shelby a temporary hideout on his ranch. But soon the sizzle between them has this wealthy cowboy wondering if seduction will convince her to stay...

Read on for a sneak peek of
Runaway Temptation
by USA TODAY *bestselling author Maureen Child, the first in the Texas Cattleman's Club: Bachelor Auction series!*

Shelby Arthur stared at her own reflection and hardly recognized herself. She supposed all brides felt like that on their wedding day, but for her, the effect was terrifying.

She was looking at a stranger wearing an old-fashioned gown with long, lacy sleeves, a cinched waist and full skirt, and a neckline that was so high she felt as if she were choking. Shelby was about to get married in a dress she hated, a veil she didn't want, to a man she wasn't sure she liked, much less loved. How did she get to this point?

"Oh, God. What am I doing?"

She'd left her home in Chicago to marry Jared Goodman. But now that he was home in Texas, under his awful father's thumb, Jared was someone she didn't

HDEXP0818

even know. Her whirlwind romance had morphed into a nightmare and now she was trapped.

Shelby met her own eyes in the mirror and read the desperation there. In a burst of fury, she ripped her veil off her face. Then, blowing a stray auburn lock from her forehead, she gathered up the skirt of the voluminous gown in both arms and hurried down the hall and toward the nearest exit.

And ran smack into a brick wall.

Well, that was what it felt like.

A tall, gorgeous brick wall who grabbed her upper arms to steady her, then smiled down at her with humor in his eyes. He had enough sex appeal to light up the city of Houston, and the heat from his hands, sliding down her body, made everything inside her jolt into life.

"Aren't you headed the wrong way?" he asked, and the soft drawl in his deep voice awakened a single thought in her mind.

Oh, boy.

Don't miss
Runaway Temptation
by USA TODAY *bestselling author Maureen Child, the first in the Texas Cattleman's Club: Bachelor Auction series.*

Available September 2018 wherever Harlequin® Desire books and ebooks are sold.

www.Harlequin.com

Copyright © 2018 by Harlequin Books S.A.

HDEXP0818

Want to give in to temptation with steamy tales of irresistible desire?

Check out **Harlequin® Presents®**, **Harlequin® Desire** and **Harlequin® Kimani™ Romance** books!

New books available every month!

CONNECT WITH US AT:

Harlequin.com/Community

 Facebook.com/HarlequinBooks

 Twitter.com/HarlequinBooks

 Instagram.com/HarlequinBooks

 Pinterest.com/HarlequinBooks

ReaderService.com

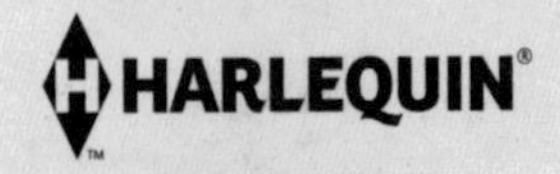

ROMANCE WHEN YOU NEED IT

PGENRE2017